I0546468

Books by Christopher Conlon

NOVELS
A Matrix of Angels
Midnight on Mourn Street

SHORT FICTION
Thundershowers at Dusk: Gothic Stories
Saying Secrets: American Stories

POETRY
Starkweather Dreams
Mary Falls: Requiem for Mrs. Surratt
The Weeping Time
Gilbert and Garbo in Love

DRAMA
Midnight on Mourn Street: A Play in Two Acts

AS EDITOR
A Sea of Alone: Poems for Alfred Hitchcock
He Is Legend: An Anthology Celebrating Richard Matheson
Poe's Lighthouse
The Twilight Zone Scripts of Jerry Sohl
Filet of Sohl

Praise for *A Matrix of Angels*

"With lean and graceful prose, Christopher Conlon takes us on a compulsive contemporary journey into memory both intensely beautiful and horrific, exploring friendship, loss, and transformation. *A Matrix of Angels* is not only a novel to savor, but one that will stick to your bones. It is also a tale that will capture the hearts and minds of mainstream readers as well as horror aficionados. Highest recommendation!"
    –Bruce Boston, author of *The Guardener's Tale* and *Dark Matters*

"Christopher Conlon does so much in the limited space of this short novel, one hardly knows where to start. To describe *A Matrix of Angels* as 'Holden Caulfield meets Thelma and Louise in Mayberry, USA—plus a visit from Hannibal Lecter' barely hints at what Conlon has accomplished. *A Matrix of Angels* is a *bildungsroman*, a nostalgic, bittersweet visit to the small town America of three decades ago, a study in sin and, if not redemption, then at least a degree of acceptance and of survival. Fran and Lucy are amazingly real and compelling characters. You will not forget this book for a very long time."
    –Richard A. Lupoff, author of *The Emerald Cat Killer* and *Killer's Dozen*

"An engrossing, literate and highly original thriller that reinvents the serial killer narrative by making the killer peripheral to the story. The real detective work here involves uncovering poignant memories of a long-past friendship, with an emphasis on deeply felt emotions rather than standard genre thrills. Conlon is a masterful writer, effortlessly interweaving stories from two different eras with prose that sings beautifully, whether he's describing childhood joys or brutal disappointments. At once devastating and life-affirming, *A Matrix of Angels* is an unforgettable experience."
    –Norman Prentiss, Bram Stoker Award-winning author of *Invisible Fences*

"Every so often a work of fiction comes along that so defies easy description or categorization that it arguably creates its own genre—works such as Philip K. Dick's *Valis* and Theodore Sturgeon's *The Dreaming Jewels* spring instantly to mind; well, you can now add Christopher Conlon's *A Matrix of Angels* to that list. By turns horrifying, poignant, baffling, tragic, dream-like, and refreshingly unsentimental in its depiction of childhood and its traumas both large and small, this novel's mind-bending and intensely introspective structure had me mesmerized from first page to last, and re-affirmed once again that Conlon's singular genius as a storyteller is a gift to those readers smart enough—and brave enough—to read his work. *A Matrix of Angels* is the work of a brilliant writer nearing the height of his considerable powers. I wish I'd written it."

–Gary A. Braunbeck, International Horror Guild and Bram Stoker Award-winning author of *To Each Their Darkness* and *A Cracked and Broken Path*

"Christopher Conlon has written another wonderful tale that's impossible to put down. As deeply flawed as his characters may be, and despite the tragedy at the heart of this tale, *A Matrix of Angels* is also a story of hope. Often dark, but ultimately uplifting and hauntingly beautiful, this is one of the best things I've read this year, without a doubt."

–James Newman, author of *Midnight Rain* and *Animosity*

A MATRIX OF ANGELS

A novel by

Christopher Conlon

A Matrix of Angels
by Christopher Conlon

ISBN-10 1894953-711
ISBN-13 978-1894953-719
Trade edition – first edition.
This book is also available as a limited edition hardcover
and in ebook editions.

Cover art: Filippino Lippi (c. 1457–1504), "The Vision of
St. Bernard" (detail).

Library and Archives Canada Cataloguing in Publication

Conlon, Christopher, 1962-
A matrix of angels / Christopher Conlon.

Issued also in an electronic format.
ISBN 978-1-894953-78-8 (bound).--ISBN 978-1-894953-
71-9 (pbk.)

I. Title.

PS3603.O559M37 2011 813'.6 C2010-906996-X

A MATRIX OF ANGELS

A novel by

Christopher Conlon

Creative Guy Publishing
Vancouver | Canada

TABLE OF CONTENTS

for Pete Allen

nothing which we are to perceive in this world equals
the power of your intense fragility:whose texture
compels me with the colour of its countries,
rendering death and forever with each breathing

—e.e. cummings

…a child's major attention has to be concentrated on
how to fit into a world which, with every passing hour,
reveals itself as merciless.

—James Baldwin

—One—

IN MY DREAM Lucy Sparrow stands facing me in the night surf, fists on her hips, waves bursting softly about her thighs, looking much as I remember her at twelve when the two of us were best friends forever: blood sisters. She wears no bathing suit, but isn't exactly naked; instead her body appears featureless, like a doll's, lacking nipples or navel, freckles or scars—incomplete, unfinished. Yet her face is as it was in life. The big raincloud-colored eyes, the shapeless nose, the tangled dirty-blonde hair splayed to her shoulders.

Little happens in the dream. She just stares at me, her expression flat, unreadable—neither friendly nor hostile—while from the shore I whisper over and over, a hot ache pulsing in my throat: *Lucy. Lucy.* But a sudden shriek overhead (a bird? a bat?) makes me flinch reflexively and I glance up in fear.

By the time I look toward her again, I'm alone in the darkness.

As I spiraled slowly toward wakefulness I turned, as I always did, to drape my arm over Donald, and was momentarily perturbed, as I always was, to find that he wasn't there. It had been two years since we'd shared a bed, yet my semi-conscious habits hadn't changed. I've read that amputees react the same way, still believing in the minutes before reality comes hammering over them that their severed limb is attached, healthy, perfectly normal. And then they wake up.

I woke up.

The room was strange. For a moment I didn't see it as a room at all, but rather as a disconnected array of random, anonymous components: desk, lamp, mirror, curtain. I had to shake my head and lift myself onto my elbows to recall that I was in a mid-priced sort of hotel in a small town called Quiet. Quiet, California, where I'd lived for some months as a girl but which was never, never home.

Depression is wonderful for sleep—for mine, anyway. It takes me into the deepest of all possible slumbers, where there's no light, no sound, no sensation, and no desire for them. Fifteen hours straight, sometimes. The only trouble is that upon waking I'm not refreshed in the least; it's almost as if I hadn't slept at all. It was that way now. I felt like dropping back to the pillow again, pulling the starch-stiffened sheets over my head and falling away from the world once more. After all, I reasoned, I was on no set schedule; the book festival in Santa Barbara had ended the day before and I had several days entirely to myself. No one needed me anywhere for anything. I was free. And so the pull of the pillow, the sheets, the warm blankets was overwhelming.

Still, I managed to sit up, stretch, wipe the muzziness from my eyes. And as I sat there, vaguely aware of the sunlight glowing through the hotel room curtains, I realized to my amazement that I had dreamed.

I never dream. I haven't since I was a child. Some brain researchers claim we all do, but that a small percentage of people like me simply don't recall them—well, it may be. What I know is that I'd never in my adult life had a dream that I remembered upon waking. The night before, for the first time, I'd had one. About Lucy.

I breathed slowly, wondering. Lucy Sparrow, of whom—until last week—I'd not had a conscious thought in thirty years. A figure I'd hurled into the black waters of oblivion three decades before. An intolerable memory. Lucy Sparrow.

I'd been sitting in my study—I work from my home, in Tucson—going over final arrangements for the festival on my laptop, re-confirming my hotel reservation and schedule, when it occurred to me that Santa Barbara wasn't all that far south of a place I'd once lived, however briefly, when I was twelve years old. How long had it been since I'd given a moment's thought to Quiet, California? And yet as soon as the name came back to me I knew that I would drive there after the event. Just to look. To see. To walk those streets again. It would be the opposite of a sentimental journey; to think of that period of my life brought me only hazy, reverberating pain, like an ancient wound freshly prodded. But I'd survived it—all of it. Quiet, California held no terrors for me. Or so I told myself.

Even then, while making new reservations and plotting my route, I didn't really think of Lucy. If she crossed the landscape of my mind at all it was only glancingly, a long-forgotten figure of no greater importance than other girls I'd known whose names now came easily back into my consciousness: Melissa Deaver, Susan Roselli, Miriam Doyle. The teachers, too. Mrs. Petrie. Mr. and Mrs. Lowther, the young couple. The principal, Mr. Blatt. And the people I lived with then, the mysterious Aunt Louise and Uncle Frank to whom I'd been shuffled off inexplicably in the middle of a rain-splintered night.

Why do I have to go, Dad?

Mom, what did I do?

All thirty years gone. I was a grown woman now with an excellent career, a mortgage. My marriage had failed, and my daughter and I rarely spoke, but I was a success by most standards. Yet I felt like something else, something that made me want to collapse back into the bed and hide myself away.

Donald, please have Jess come to the phone.
I've tried, Frances. She refuses. I can't physically drag her.
I have a right to speak to my daughter, Donald!
Your daughter is in her bedroom crying, Frances.

I threw my legs over the bed, determined to stand. It was puzzling that I was nude; I'm not in the habit of sleeping nude. No one was with me, certainly. But then I noticed the bottle of Calvert's whiskey on the side table, the partly-full glass, the bucket of water which last night had likely been ice. It came back to me, dimly. I'd decided, after an hour or two of TV and drinking, to take a shower, but had fallen asleep instead…

Passed out, my mind amended.

Of course I'm aware of the irony: a melancholic divorcee with a drinking problem and a daughter who doesn't speak to her making her living—and it's a good living—as a creator of children's books. What would the second-graders of the world think, I wondered, if they could see me now—the celebrated lady who wrote and illustrated the stories of Flat-Head Fred and Mary the Motor Scooter?

I noticed that I'd left one of my titles, *Mary's Trip to Muffin Land,* on the side table, its back cover facing up. There I was in a little photo in the corner, full color, an attractive but somewhat hysterical-looking woman wearing too much makeup (what *had* I been thinking with that eyeliner?) and obviously fake blonde highlights in her otherwise nondescript, practically colorless hair. What saved the image was the smile, all dimples and glossy lips and big shining teeth. People often refer to my smile. Even the man who'd introduced me at the festival used the old cringe-inducing "lights up a room" line about it. I could observe that quality in the cover photo, but it seemed to have nothing to do with me. What I mostly saw when I looked at that picture was a woman who was hiding— behind makeup, hair dye, a "dazzling" smile, but hiding just as surely as I wanted to hide now, by throwing the bedclothes over myself and sinking back into oblivion.

I have visitation rights, you know, Donald.

No one has stopped you from visiting with Jess.

Yes, under your watchful eye, right? Like I'm some kind of criminal!

I poured half an inch of last night's libation into the glass and tossed it back. Then I stood, determined to face the day like any other grown-up person. I showered, threw on jeans, T-shirt, sneakers—it was a lovely spring day, warm, sun-rich—and, after munching on an apple and banana I'd brought with me, headed downstairs, through the lobby, and out into the town of Quiet, California.

I'd not really seen it the night before. I'd arrived late, tired from the festival (all those mothers beaming at the celebrated Ms. Pastan, thanking me for getting their children interested in reading) and the drive. I'd done nothing but go straight to my room after checking in. But now here I was, on streets I'd not walked since I was twelve years old.

It would be nice to report that a bracing wave of nostalgia overwhelmed me immediately, but the fact is that I recognized nothing I saw. I crossed the parking lot and peered up and down the four-lane road before me (its creative name was "Main Street") and tried to think of what had been here thirty years earlier. But in the face of the traffic—there was a tremendous lot of it for what was supposed to still be a small town—and the shopping center across the way with its Burger King, its Starbucks, its K-Mart, I couldn't think. Of course it didn't help that I'd not lived here long; in terms of time, Quiet represented hardly a feeble dot on my personal radar screen, even if in memory it occupied a much larger (if unvisited) space. Yet I knew I would remember if I could simply get my bearings, so I turned back to the hotel office for a map of the town.

Now, searching up and down Main Street, it began to come back to me. Nothing was familiar, but with the help of the map I managed to orient myself: turning left on Main Street, I saw, led to a branch called Bridgewater Avenue (it literally included a bridge) which connected finally to the housing tract where I'd lived. There it was: Riverfield Road. I even knew the number still: 319. In the other direction were more places I recalled—the library, the elementary school—but those could wait. The distance to my old house was only a mile, so rather than using the car I started to walk. Drinking problem aside, I try to keep myself in shape.

The map indicated that Quiet, California was "A Great Place to Raise a Child," a "Thriving Community of Five Thousand and Growing!" I could remember the old sign at the city limits, *Quiet. Pop. 750.* Looking around at the bustling conglomeration of stores and stoplights the town had become I felt like a relic from another century, which of course is exactly what I was. It seemed a pleasant place really, clean, modern, clearly affluent, yet faceless, without character; it might have been a mid-sized village anywhere in the country. Only the tall palm trees lining the roadway betrayed its California setting.

When I reached Bridgewater Avenue, however, things changed. Here there had been almost no development—there was little I didn't seem to recognize in approaching the bridge, and as I walked out onto its two-lane span, I realized that it was the same bridge I'd ridden across on the school bus, that I'd walked and run and biked over countless times. It hadn't altered, hadn't been widened or rebuilt. I knew it immediately. What an unsettling feeling to stand on it again, to look down at the dry riverbed a hundred feet below and see that it hadn't changed either. No new housing, no business development; just a riverbed of dirt, rocks, and wild grasses where once, many years ago, millions of gallons of water had rushed headlong toward the sea.

A large truck swooshed past, its blast of air pushing at me like a pair of hard hands. At the same moment a memory stabbed into my mind, making me gasp. My breath came fast and shallow. I felt dizzy. Blinking rapidly, I leaned over the safety rail, fearful I was about to throw up.

Quiet, California. A Great Place to Raise a Child.

Was that line meant as a sick joke?

I inhaled deeply, slowly exhaled. I closed my eyes for a moment, regaining my balance. My head throbbed. There was a sour taste in my throat. I was hardly aware of the traffic passing by each way on the bridge.

A great place to raise a child.

Quiet, California held no terrors for me, I kept telling myself. No terrors at all.

I knew the house at once, though its color had gone from yellow to blue and the pitted asphalt of the old driveway had been replaced with smooth white concrete. There were perky green bushes lining the walkway to the door now, and the door itself was different, imposing polished oak. But these changes were trivial. It was the same long, low house in which I'd once lived, a California rambler much like many others on this street.

The neighborhood itself, like the town, had clearly undergone something of a renaissance. Each house in my range of vision seemed bigger, brighter, better maintained than it had been back then. Looking carefully I realized that many of the houses actually were larger, with additions in the back or on the side which I knew hadn't been there in my time. None of the cars in the driveways were more than two or three years old. The lawns were immaculate. It was not a rich person's neighborhood, but it had become comfortably well off.

Naturally it had crossed my mind to wonder whether Uncle Frank and Aunt Louise might still live here; I'd had no contact with them since the day I left the house forever, when I wasn't yet thirteen. But it was unlikely. They'd been in their mid-fifties, and neither had seemed in robust health. I could hardly imagine that the two of them, well into their eighties, might be sitting in the house at that exact moment—Frank reading his newspaper barefoot in his shirtless suspenders and Louise watching her game shows on television with a Marlboro in one hand and a can of Budweiser in the other.

I stood staring at this house of remembered pain for a long time. Finally I mounted the walkway and moved to the front door, knocked.

No answer.

I backed away. Glancing about a bit nervously, making sure no neighbors were looking through their window curtains at me, I stepped across the lawn, around the side of the house, and looked quickly into the backyard. An unfamiliar patio was there now: smooth concrete, outdoor furniture, children's toys, a grill. It looked, I thought, very pleasant, but it had nothing to do with anything I recalled. My eyes moved to the back of the lawn, near the fence. A small flowerbed huddled there; I was shocked to discover that the big old leafy pepper tree was gone, as if it had never existed. I had spent endless hours under that tree; it was a separate world from the grim one in which I lived.

Finally I looked at the back of the house itself, beheld the familiar rear window which led to what had been my bedroom. I was surprised at how small that window really was. I remembered sliding it open one spring night thirty years ago, climbing out of it. This was the window I'd used to run away. Not from home: 319 Riverfield Road was never my home. To run away, that's all.

I stepped close to it, knowing I'd best move quickly; famous children's author Frances Pastan didn't need to get arrested for trespassing. The blinds were closed (blinds, I noticed, not curtains, as I'd had); I couldn't see in at all. As I stood on the concrete that had once been grass outside what had once been my window, I touched the exterior window sill, passed my hand briefly along the wall. Here, I thought. I did it right here.

And she...she stood...

I wouldn't think of it.

I made my way to the front of the house again, stepped back onto the public sidewalk. I stood looking at the house for a long moment, uneasy washes of emotion coursing through me. At last I turned to take in the house across the street: 320. I inhaled sharply when I realized that it wasn't the same house that I knew from back then. What had been there was another rambler, not substantially different from my own house except that it was considerably more run-down, even dilapidated; no, what I was seeing now was a completely different structure, a large and lovely two-story home with big windows and a front lawn so velvety smooth that it looked like Astroturf. At some point in the past thirty years they'd demolished the old house. Literally taken a wrecking ball to it. Destroyed it. The thought made me sad, though I couldn't have said why.

I walked a few yards along the sidewalk until I reached the spot that I recalled as the school bus stop.

I looked at the two houses, my own and the one that, once upon a time, had been a different building entirely. The sun was high and bright, just as it was all those years ago when I'd stood here filled with terror at the prospect of my first day at the new school; just as it was when I heard the door across the street slam and saw the big blonde girl in T-shirt and blue jeans come careening pell-mell across the way to catch the bus. The sun was high and bright that day, that first day when I learned that the girl's name was Lucy Sparrow, two months before she was murdered.

—Two—

IT WAS MARCH. I stood in my pink cardigan and powder-blue skirt, clutching my lunch bag tightly before me in both hands and trying not to tremble. Hardly more than a week before I'd been home in Fresno, where everything was as usual; then the rain, the darkness, the eerie bus ride into the netherworld, where I was cut off from anything I'd ever known, everything I was.

Why do I have to go, Dad?

Mom, what did I do?

I had no memory of Uncle Frank or Aunt Louise, though in helping me board my mother had assured me I would remember these people as soon as I saw them. "You knew them when you were little, honey," she said, which might have been the case, but I certainly didn't recognize them when I got there. I wasn't even clear how either of them was related to my parents.

That bus ride: a nightmarish succession of headlights slashing by in the rain, the blackness of open country followed by a small town's gleaming lights which shone meltingly through the wet windows. It seemed endless, terrifying, though I was even more fearful of what would happen when it ended. Where would I be? How would I live? Would I ever find my way home?

These events had only just happened when I found myself standing one morning where I'd been told to stand to wait for the bus, holding desperately to my lunch bag as if it were a life preserver in the midst of tempest-tossed seas. I held myself rigidly still, thinking, *School, school, it's time to go to school, I must go to school,* trying to forget that I was a stranger among strangers, that I had no idea where I was or why. What was Quiet, California to me? I couldn't have found it on a map to save my soul. And yet school—yes!—school would make me normal again, give me an identity, it would make me a *person,* so unlike what I was now, which was nothing.

Just as the bus came rumbling up the street I heard the door across the way burst open and then immediately slam shut again. A girl about my age came charging into the road toward me, running recklessly in front of the bus as it braked to a stop. She wore a dirty black T-shirt emblazoned with the words *Bachman-Turner Overdrive* along with tattered blue jeans and sneakers. There was a backpack slung sloppily over her shoulder.

"Hi," she said breathlessly, without looking at me. She was taller than I, bigger, with blonde hair that looked like it hadn't been brushed that morning, perhaps for several mornings. As the bus door swung open she said, "You new here?"

I nodded wordlessly.

"Hm." She looked me up and down dubiously, clearly finding fault with my cardigan and skirt. As she turned to mount the bus steps I heard the harsh voice of the driver instructing her to never run in front of the bus. "Aw, c'mon, Mr. Cox," she said, stepping up into the vehicle, "you were stopping anyway, right? I knew you weren't gonna run me over." I followed her up the steps.

"Young lady," he said—I could see now that Mr. Cox was a burly, graying man with pockmarked skin—"I have to tell your mother if you keep doing it. Stop it, now."

To my surprise she turned back to me suddenly and whispered, "You gotta love a guy named *Cox,*" then giggled and moved down the aisle.

The bus was mercifully empty, or nearly so. I dropped myself into the seat behind the girl's and wondered how long the ride would be. As the bus pulled out, she again looked at me. She said, in conspiratorially low tones: "Guess what his *first* name is."

"Whose?"

"The bus driver's, stupid."

I shrugged, shook my head.

She grinned. "It's *Dick*," she said. "Can you believe that? The bus driver's name is *Dick Cox*." She laughed, a big, throaty laugh not unlike a bark. I smiled again, politely, unaware of why all this was so humorous. She scowled at me suddenly. "You get it," she said, "don't you?"

I squirmed uncomfortably in my seat. "Sure. I get it."

"Then why aren't you laughing?"

"I just don't think it's that funny."

She looked suspicious. "Okay, then, what's the joke?"

"The joke?"

"Dick Cox. What's the joke with that name?"

"I—" I looked down, fidgeted with my lunch bag. "It—it sounds funny."

I could feel this big blonde girl, heavyset, not pretty, studying me.

"'It sounds funny,'" she repeated.

I stayed silent, hoping something would distract her attention. Please leave me alone, I wanted to say. Just leave me alone.

"It's because they're both names for a boy's private parts," she said finally, taking pity on me. "Dick? Cox? Get it?"

I didn't respond. I was twisting the edge of my cardigan in my fingers, unable to stop.

"I don't like that sweater," she said, eying me critically. "It's too girlie. Anyway, what are you wearing a sweater for?

It's not cold."

"I—get cold a lot," I said meekly, which was the truth.

"Yeah? I don't get cold at all, hardly. Why do you wear your hair in bangs like that?"

"I don't know."

"Kinda nerdy."

I stared out the bus window. We were heading across the bridge that separated the housing tract from the downtown. It was a long drop from the bridge to the riverbed below, I saw, long enough to kill a person if they wanted to jump.

"What's your name?" the girl demanded.

"Frances."

"What?"

"*Frances*," I said, louder this time. "Frances Pastan."

"Frances." She considered it. "Fran."

I shook my head. "Nobody calls me Fran."

"Well, they should. Like Fran Tarkington. He's a football player. You heard of him?"

I shook my head again.

"Well, you should've," she said. "He's a quarterback. Minnesota Vikings."

I nodded.

"Lucy," she said finally.

"What?"

"Lucy, stupid. My name. Lucy. Lucy Sparrow."

"Oh." I nodded again.

"You just moved in, didn't you?"

"Yes."

"Are the Cartmills your parents?"

The bus was pulling up to a sidewalk where a large group of children was waiting, at least a dozen of them.

"I *said*," she repeated, looking at me in annoyance, "are the Cartmills your parents?"

I twisted the cardigan, twisted it, twisted it. "No," I whispered. At last I looked at her. "Would you—would you please not talk to me?"

She stared at me as the bus filled with noisy girls and boys. I noticed her unusual eyes, gray with a hint of silver; her flat nose, her thin, rather chapped lips. She had a birthmark, I saw, a narrow brown line running from the corner of her jaw down to the mid-point of her neck.

"Crap," she said, as the bus began to move again, "are you crying?"

I suddenly realized that I was. Shame-faced, I wiped my eyes with my palms.

I'd feared she would laugh at me for my tears, but to my surprise she didn't. Instead she studied me closely.

"Not your parents, huh?" she said thoughtfully.

I shook my head.

"Well, crap," she said. "That sucks."

We had the same homeroom together, as well as most of our classes, but Lucy and I didn't speak again until lunchtime. In the meanwhile I sat in the back of each classroom, eyes firmly on my desk, saying nothing to anyone. Books were issued to me and placed in my hands; I only opened them if the teacher instructed the class to do so. Although Quiet itself was so small as to be practically nonexistent, Soames Elementary School took in students from several neighboring towns, so there were fifteen or twenty students in each class. After a simple greeting from each teacher at the beginning of the period I was, for the most part, blessedly ignored. Many of us traveled together from classroom to classroom—I could feel the eyes of the other girls analyzing, evaluating me; and already I could sense that I was coming up short to the ones who really mattered, the girls I was able to identify before we were even done with first period. Melissa Deaver, Susan Roselli, Miriam Doyle. The pretty ones, the popular ones without whose approval no girl would ever be really important in the school. I must have seemed hopeless to them, drab as I was, shy and silent; at morning recess, during which I sat alone under a tree, I saw them across the playground studying me, their lovely but cruel faces huddled together. At last one of them—it was Miriam Doyle, all sleek black hair and premature bust—made her way over to me, clearly an emissary sent to test the waters. She said hi, introduced herself, asked me a few questions about who I was, where I was from. My answers were monosyllabic; I made no eye contact. After two or three minutes of this torture—and it was torture for both of us, I'm sure, not just me—Miriam smiled, said, "Okay, 'bye," and skipped back over to her friends.

When the bell rang and we shuffled toward class again I heard her in front of me, giggling to Melissa and Susan: the phrase *total zombie* floated through the air to my ears, and I knew that I'd failed their test, the only one that counted. We weren't even through morning classes yet, and my place in the pecking order had already been invincibly determined.

Lunch, however, was a different story. I sat with my brown bag on the grass not far from the school building, next to the little kids' playground: designed for the smaller children, from whom we were segregated (they took their lunch before us), it contained a swing set, sandbox, a jungle gym. The older kids never used this equipment; it was considered beneath their dignity. Instead the boys hustled about with their footballs and basketballs while the girls lounged around under the trees or hit tennis balls at each other on the school courts, this being the era of the tennis craze spawned by Jimmy Connors and Chris Evert.

Yet on the little kids' playground there was one girl who was pounding a tetherball with great energy. She hit it with enormous power, sending the ball in wild circles and then smashing it again in the other direction, grunting each time, her hair flying in the breeze. It was the girl from the bus. Lucy.

Eventually she noticed me. "Hey," she said.

I clutched at my lunch bag, looked away.

"Aren't you gonna eat?" she called to me, pounding at the tetherball again.

I glanced down at the bag, trying to think of a response. I didn't know what was in the bag—Aunt Louise had packed it and shoved it into my hands that morning—and I found myself afraid to open it. Whatever it was, disgusting or delicious, it would be different from what Alba, our maid, had habitually prepared, and I felt somehow that I'd had enough difference for one day, that if one more different thing happened to me I might shatter into pieces.

"I'm not hungry," I said finally.

"Not *hungry*?" She let the ball go and came near me, looming over me, blotting out the sun. "What do you mean, you're not hungry?"

"I'm just—not." I held it out to her. "Do you want it?"

She eyed the bag appraisingly. "Well, maybe," she said. "What've you got?"

I shrugged. "I don't know."

She scowled and dropped down next to me. "Here, let's see it." Taking the bag, she opened it, peered inside, and began pulling things from it. "Sandwich…peanut butter. Little thing of orange juice. Apple…Hey, there's some cookies in here!" She pulled them out: two Oreos in a clear plastic sack.

"Now, c'mon," she said. "I *know* you want these. Anybody who doesn't like Oreos is a crazy person. You're not a crazy person, are you?" She held out a cookie to me.

Actually, I wasn't—Oreos were something that Alba might have packed, so I took the cookie. "Thanks," I said, biting down.

"Hey, it's your lunch. Do you mind if I have the other one?"

"No." I shook my head. "I mean, yes. I mean, go ahead."

We sat there in the sunshine. I watched her work on her Oreo, pulling it apart and scraping away the white filling with her teeth before munching on the dark cookie halves. Then she bit into the apple.

"First day can be hard," she said, chewing.

I didn't respond.

"I've only been here since the start of the year," she said. "So I was the new kid in September. This school isn't too bad, I guess. But there are some bitches here you should stay away from." She pointed across the green lawn to the place where Melissa, Susan, and Miriam were huddled together, giggling. "Hey," she said, jumping up, "you want to play tetherball?"

I looked away, shook my head.

"Aw, come *on*," she insisted, leaning down and grabbing my arm. "It'll be fun."

"I don't *want* to."

She stood again, looked at me. "Well, okay. Thanks for the lunch."

She moved off to the tetherball pole again, took the ball in her left hand and then whacked at it with her right. The ball spun. I watched this loud, blowsy girl focus her entire attention on the tetherball, as if her life depended on giving it a solid smash every single time. Glancing across the grass I saw Melissa, Susan, and Miriam pointing and laughing openly now—laughing at her. I couldn't hear their words but I could imagine them easily enough: *What a pig, can you believe she plays on the little kids' playground, she's so gross!* They themselves were pretty, all three of them. Melissa was a twelve-year-old version of a California beach blonde, with blue eyes and perky upturned nose. Susan was a dark-featured Italian bombshell. Miriam, the plainest of the three, made up for her lack of facial beauty with a sensationally curvaceous body years ahead of its time. All their clothes were immaculate, fresh clean jeans and skirts with tops that fit them as if they'd been custom tailored. Their hair was meticulously groomed and held with fancy ribbons and barrettes. They wore shiny bracelets and rings.

Lucy Sparrow had none of these things. She was a large-framed kid who was well on her way to being fat. Her cheeks were spotted with freckles. Her clothes were old, torn, and as she swung at the tetherball I could see the dark stains under her arms. When she'd been sitting next to me I could smell her—a sweat odor, a girl-smell no doubt offensive to the delicate ethereal creatures across the lawn. Suddenly, in a rush of hot anger, I hated them. I pictured myself marching across the lawn and kicking their faces in, slapping at them, dragging them by their precious hair and smashing their heads against the school's wall.

Instead I picked up the remnants of my lunch and threw them in the trash bin. Then I walked hesitantly toward Lucy.

She seemed unsurprised. "Here," she said, sending the ball practically into orbit. "Get this one."

I was a hopeless maladroit, however, and in my first attempt I completely missed; I swung at nothing but air. I heard the girls laugh.

Suddenly Lucy grabbed the ball, glancing at them but then looking steadily at me. "You're off balance," she said, "and you're not keeping your eye on it. Look." She stood with her legs apart, bounced a bit this way and that. "See, you can keep your balance this way. And *look* at the ball. You'll hit it if you don't take your eye off it. Here, try."

She lofted the ball gently at me. I swung, and to my surprise I hit it—poorly, but I hit it. The ball skittered off in the wrong direction.

"That's better," she said. "Try again. And plant your feet the way I showed you. Like this. Yeah, that's good. But you gotta close your fist, like this, see? Otherwise you're just slapping at it. Here, try again." She tossed the ball at me and I swung, making solid contact. "Hey, yeah, that's it," she said, tracking the flight of the ball and then capturing it again. "Here, let's practice."

And for the next several minutes she coached me, my aim and swing quickly improving. At last we began playing together, she socking it hard—though not nearly as hard as she'd been doing before—and I sending it back the other way as best I could. When the bell rang for afternoon classes I realized to my shock that I had actually been having fun.

"What's your next class?" Lucy asked, as we gave the ball a few more punches.

"I think it's…Social Studies?" I said, swinging.

"We're together, then. Mr. Lowther. He's pretty cool. He tells good stories. I like him better than his wife. She teaches Science."

I hardly heard what she was saying, however, after the words *We're together, then.* I realized that we had all but one morning class together, too. I was suddenly thrilled.

We talked of teachers and classes while banging at the tetherball, hardly noticing that most of the other students had disappeared from the playground. Finally Mrs. Petrie's voice broke in from across the lawn, calling, "Lucy! Frances! Time for class!" and we looked at each other, laughing for no particular reason.

I started to turn toward the school, but Lucy said, "Wait a sec," and grabbed the ball again. She made a determined face, breathed hard for effect, and as she struck powerfully at the ball she grunted, "That's for Melissa-the-Bitch *Deaver*!" She grabbed the ball as it came around, socked it again: "And that's for Susan-the-Bitch *Roselli*!" A final time: "And that's for Miriam-the-Bitch *Doyle*!" Watching the tetherball swing wildly around the pole, I was giddy with excitement and a sense of mischief, danger.

My breath came short as I cried impulsively, "They're *bitches*!"

Lucy looked at me, shocked; then she laughed. I guessed why: there I stood, small, shy, mousy in my cardigan and skirt, a nondescript little girl swearing at the top of her lungs.

"C'mon," she said, smiling, "we gotta go in."

Giggling, we ran hand-in-hand across the grass.

—Three—

THIRTY YEARS LATER I was surprised to discover that Soames Elementary hadn't really changed. Like my old house, of course, it seemed smaller, differently-dimensioned; but the buildings and corridors were all instantly familiar to me. It was a Saturday, so the place was deserted; I could hardly help but feel a certain level of melancholy as I ambled past old familiar windows and doors in what seemed a lifeless universe. I peered into Room 10, Mr. Lowther's old room, and wondered who taught there now. I leaned down to the oddly low drinking fountain outside what had been Mrs. Petrie's room, took a sip of lukewarm water. A breeze blew a stray sheet of paper along the side of the building. There was no one near, no one at all.

I made my way out onto the grass behind the school, where the playground still stood. There was a big blue building off to my left which I'd never seen; I wondered what it was. Part of the big open area in back had been converted into a softball field, I saw, complete with pitcher's mound and dirt base paths and a protective fence behind home plate. Beyond the grass, in the fields behind the school's property, there were a few more houses than there had been. But again, it was all recognizable, and this surprised me, even depressed me somehow.

Finally I walked toward what we'd thought of as the little kids' playground and saw that it still contained swings and sandbox, though the jungle gym wasn't the same; it was a bigger, brighter structure before me now, clearly made or at least coated with some substance other than the solid steel

I recalled. It stood dully in the spring light, no doubt less dangerous than the old metal contraption I remembered, yet curiously uninviting.

At last I wandered to where the tetherball pole had stood, and found to my amazement that it was still there. Not the same pole, certainly—this looked far too bright and polished to have been here for more than three decades. But that this particular intersection of space and time still held a tetherball pole: the fact was incredible to me.

No tetherball, however. A cord for one dangled listlessly against the pole, but where the ball should have been there was only empty space. I looked across the grass, felt the strange sensation of somehow being in two places at the same time—or rather different times. The little girl I'd been suddenly felt very close. A wave of emotion coursed through me, though I couldn't have named what I felt. After a moment it passed, leaving me alone in the bright sun.

It was in the town library that I began to understand the real reason I'd returned to Quiet, California.

The library itself had been completely remodeled; once past the familiar Victorian-style exterior, I would never have known where I was. Gone was the crepuscular darkness of the building I recalled, with its echoing hardwood floors and dim reading lamps and huge card catalog standing like a sentinel by the front door. The old-fashioned leather-bound chairs with their hard brass brads were nowhere in evidence. Instead this was a sunny, cheery room with big windows, lightweight portable furniture, color-splashed posters, and glowing computers lining the walls.

The rosy-cheeked woman behind the desk was extremely helpful. She was perhaps ten years younger than I and looked younger still in her bright yellow sun dress. She was fascinated to learn how long ago I'd lived here and claimed to remember Frank and Louise Cartmill, though I couldn't imagine how since I'd never seen either of them with a book. She told me that Mrs. Klibo—the librarian I'd known—had passed away fifteen years before.

"And what do you do, now?" she asked, smiling, friendly.

"Children's books," I told her, without elaborating. I didn't mention that several of them were on her shelves. "I was wondering," I asked, "what information you might have about the Riverbed Killer."

I dislike clichés, but it was a fact: her face fell.

"Oh," she said. "Of course."

I realized instantly that the Riverbed Killer must still be a sore point with the locals of Quiet, California. In a way this was strange. He was hardly famous; in fact, he was entirely forgotten except by the handful of ghouls who study such people. He certainly wasn't remembered in the way that others were—Starkweather, Whitman, Bundy, Dahmer. In comparison to them he was a small-timer. He claimed, after all, only three victims, hardly enough by the 1970s to even make the national news. Still, I found myself wondering how many more people had ever been murdered in this little town and its environs in the decades since. Few, certainly; quite possibly none. And so his notoriety here had gone on, though I suspect he was rarely mentioned in conversation today.

"What did you want to know?" she asked, her demeanor notably cooler now.

"Well—you see, I knew one of his victims."

She cocked her head. "Did you?" Sympathy returned to her voice.

I nodded. "The last one. Lucy Sparrow."

"Lucy Sparrow." She seemed to think about it. "The name

sounds familiar."

"Yes, well…she was the last."

"And you knew her."

I nodded again. "I knew him, too."

"McCoy?"

"Yes." I could picture him now, the red-veined black eyes, the jumbled teeth. "But I didn't know him well. Lucy—actually, she was my best friend."

This brought the woman completely back to my side. "Oh," she said, her face stricken, "I'm so sorry."

Thirty years later, and she still expressed sympathy. As well, perhaps, she might: for it never goes away. It just goes dormant. It hides. It hid in me for three decades at the bottom of a deep pool of feeling and memory that had been, or seemed, placid and peaceful. But something had happened when I began to think of Quiet, California again: the pool had begun to stir, the waters to thrash and heave. And when I arrived here things I'd forgotten, things that I never knew I remembered at all, began to surface, chief among them the ghastly, intolerable thought, the unresolved grief and rage of knowing that Lucy shouldn't have died. That I had a chance to save her—and failed.

"I'm wondering if you have much information about the case," I said. "I've looked online. There isn't a lot there." I'd found his picture on a few sites devoted to serial killers, along with a basic paragraph here and there describing his crimes and listing the victims: Maria Sanchez, Trista Blake, Lucille Sparrow. There was one website that had images of each girl, pixilated black-and-whites obviously reproduced from newspapers of the time, and there she was, Lucy, in what looked to be a school portrait, her long hair brushed back off her forehead, tidier than it usually was, her smile big and crooked. It was the first time I'd seen her face in all those decades. She looked younger than I remembered her, of course. She looked like what she'd been. A child.

"Well," the librarian said, "we have our old microfilm files. You could look up the *News-Press* articles from back then. It might take some time."

"I've got time."

She led me into a separate small room which contained nothing but a single aged microfilm machine and row upon row of file cabinets, each of which contained little indexed spools of film.

"I'm afraid nobody comes in here anymore," she said. "Everything's a bit dusty. Do you know how to work the machine?"

I nodded, smiling. "Graduate school."

The day was quiet in the library, only a few children returning overdue books and a patron or two using the computers, so she stayed with me for a while, helping me isolate dates and spool up some of the film strips. The images blurred by on the illuminated screen: lots of Nixon, Kissinger, Vietnam, Ford. But she knew the dates I was looking for, and quickly found the first headline: *Local Girl Missing*. This was the Maria Sanchez case. I remembered it vaguely. She was a high school girl who had vanished; at first, I recalled, her boyfriend was considered the prime suspect. It came back to me as I read. Then, a month later: *Girl's Remains Found*. In the riverbed, almost directly under the bridge. Only a day or two after that, *Another Girl Missing*. Trista Blake, a second high-schooler. The police swarmed the riverbed, of course, and found her quickly, about a mile north of Maria Sanchez's body.

My heart was slamming against my chest as we came to the next headline, which I'd never seen. *Third Girl Missing*. And then: *Third Girl's Body Located Outside Town*. There:

Lucy Sparrow, twelve, the youngest and final victim, was found "scattered across a wide area" in the riverbed south of town among the wild grasses and mud. She was chopped into pieces. Her head was drilled full of holes.

I continued to read, engrossed by article after article. It almost seemed as if this story had nothing to do with me or anyone I'd ever known. Had I really lived here? Had I actually known one of the victims? The events of thirty years past had taken on a legendary quality in my mind, as if they were things I remembered from a storybook I'd once read. Later news items headlined the investigation: *Local Mechanic Michael McCoy Arrested in Murders,* announced the most important of these. But of course, I was long gone from Quiet, California by then.

"Excuse me?" It was the librarian, behind me in the doorway. "I'm sorry, but we're closing now. We close at one o'clock on Saturdays."

I exhaled, staring at the screen, tiredness suddenly overcoming me. I'd been sitting here for nearly two hours.

"Did you find what you were looking for?" she asked.

I stood, stretched, began putting away the last microfilm reel. "I don't know," I admitted. "I'm not sure what I was looking for. But you've been very helpful."

She smiled as she went back to the main room, gently herded children toward the door. At last, packed and ready, I headed toward the exit myself.

"You know," she said, "his sister still lives around here. Sarah."

"McCoy's sister?"

She nodded, eyes toward the floor.

"I don't think I knew he had one," I said.

"She lives out on Blackstone Road." She gestured vaguely. "Ten miles or so out of town. She has a different name. Shaw.

Her husband died a few years ago."

"How interesting," I said, neutrally.

"I'm sorry you couldn't have come back for a happier reason," she said, smiling sadly at me.

"So am I, yes. Well…thank you again."

I walked down the steps, hearing her shut and lock the door behind me. Then I turned to take another look at the familiar old Victorian façade, carefully repeating to myself: *Sarah Shaw. Blackstone Road. Sarah Shaw. Blackstone Road.*

Yes: I was beginning to understand the real reason I'd returned to Quiet, California.

—Four—

FROM THAT DAY forward, in the mercurial way of young girls, Lucy and I were best friends. I could hardly believe it. I'd never been one to make friends easily; I was always the one that my peers derided as *Stuck-Up Girl, Miss Prissy Face, Full-of-Herself Frances.* My clothes were weirdly formal for someone my age, little blouses and cardigans, skirts, perfectly-shined shoes; never for me the blue jeans or T-shirts or sneakers of other kids. I rarely spoke to anyone, and when I did I was aware of a tone in my voice that was remote, almost cold, though I didn't mean it to be. At my old school, in my old life hundreds of miles from Soames Elementary, I was in the habit of spending my recesses and lunch periods entirely alone, sitting under a familiar oak tree with my latest book from the library, often Nancy Drew or the Hardy Boys or Alfred Hitchcock and the Three Investigators, books I was always careful with, never underlining or dog-earing a page. I was so fastidious that sometimes I couldn't begin reading at all if I found that I didn't have a proper bookmark with me.

My room at home had been the same way. My bed was always perfectly made, my desk immaculate with its textbooks carefully stacked by size next to the jar of flawlessly sharpened pencils. In my closet, all was order: formal dresses on the left, skirts next, then blouses and other tops, and finally my coat and sweaters. Beneath them sat, in militarily-precise lines, my shoes. I would habitually organize these things, along with the underclothes and more casual items in my bureau. It gave me satisfaction and comfort to see the shoes a bit straighter than before, my panties folded more crisply. It took my mind off the screaming and crashing noises that reverberated throughout the rest of the house.

I'd re-created that room here. The room itself was smaller; the desk I'd been given was older and rather scratched, and the bed sagged; but as much as I could I'd gathered together a duplicate of my bedroom at home. Like at home, I had my own bathroom next door; it too was kept spotlessly, obsessively clean.

"Never seen a kid act like her before," I overheard my Uncle Frank say once, in his roughhewn smoker's voice. It wasn't a compliment.

The rest of the house was, however, a complete contrast to my real home. There we'd had two stories, polished banisters, shining floors, Alba the maid; here everything was reduced. The rooms were small, the furnishings cheap. My aunt and uncle habitually kept the curtains closed all throughout the house, so that everything was bathed in a perpetual semi-twilight. And it was quiet. The only sound would come from Louise watching her game shows at a low volume in the afternoon with her beer and cigarettes or the rustle of Frank's newspaper, which he sat reading in shirtless suspenders while puffing on short, squat cigars. Neither of them worked—the word *disability* was spoken on occasion—so they were both there most of the time, silently shambling from room to dark room, speaking in murmurs, dully living out their days.

What a contrast to Lucy's house too, but in the opposite way. Uncle Frank and Aunt Louise, though no great shakes as home owners, kept their home and property in respectable condition; Lucy's place was something else entirely. The house itself, also a rambler, had splintered and broken woodwork everywhere; the paint was flaking off large parts of the front—you could actually see piles of old gray paint chips lying in the dirt where they'd fallen. One window was cracked and repaired with electrician's tape. Tiles were missing from the roof. The front lawn was like a battlefield, the lawn itself mostly pitted holes of dirt. Old tires were scattered aimlessly about, milk crates, a baseball bat in two pieces. The driveway was oil-spattered and crumbling.

Inside was the same. The first time I entered the house— the day we met, the day we socked the tetherball together and made fun of the popular girls—I experienced a very nearly sexual thrill at beholding how Lucy lived. I'd never seen anything like it. The carpeting was dirty, even burned in spots. Clothes, Lucy's and her mother's, lay strewn everywhere. The kitchen table was covered with spilled Cheerios. Plates and dishes covered with crumbs and time-stiffened sauces were in the sink, on the countertops, on miscellaneous tables and shelves throughout the house, with lines of ants marching to and from many of them. Though the house represented the opposite of how I lived, how I thought I *wanted* to live, I loved it immediately; loved the grime, the filth, the slovenliness of it. It seemed raunchy somehow, and thrilling as a result.

"C'mon, catch!" Lucy cried, grabbing a spongy Nerf football off a living room chair and tossing it to me.

"Lucy," I said, "who's here? Is your mom here?"

"Nah," she said casually, catching the red-and-yellow ball as I threw it back to her. "She's at work. Gets home in a couple of hours."

I was shocked. For all the madness that had occurred in my home, there had always been someone there when I arrived after school, if only Alba. Lucy was *alone*.

"We could go to my house," I said, the ball flying into my arms again. "My aunt and uncle are there."

"Why?" she said. "That's a stupid idea."

That day we played catch (*in the living room,* I kept thinking, amazed), drank Cokes, and waded around in Lucy's bedroom, which if anything was even more dramatically chaotic than the rest of the house. Her clothes covered the bed, the desk, the carpet. A Nerf basketball hoop stood crookedly in the corner, a lone blue sock dangling from it. Stuffed animals littered the floor. And she had a huge number of records, all 45 rpm singles, in collapsing piles everywhere.

"Hey, let's get some music going in here," she said enthusiastically, pushing away a shirt and bra (*She wears a bra!* I thought) to reveal a little record player on a table in the corner. "My mom gets these from the Yellow Jacket," she said, flipping through the records. "From the juke box. When they get new ones they just throw the old ones away, so my mom gets 'em for me." She dropped to the floor on her knees, searching. "Hm…The only problem is that they're kinda old, you know? But I have a radio, too, to hear the new stuff. Do you listen to the *America's Top Forty*?"

"What's that?"

"The show. With Casey Kasem? It's on every Saturday morning, nine to noon."

"I—no."

She made a sour face. "Fran, you're really out of it, you know that? I need to teach you up."

"I'm sorry."

"What are you standing there for, anyway? You look like you got a bus to catch or something. Help me find 'Frankenstein.'"

I knelt beside her, picked up a few of the records and looked at their titles. At twelve I was only vaguely aware of pop music; none of the names looked familiar to me.

"What's the Yellow Jacket?" I asked finally.

"That's the bar where my mom works. It's downtown. She's a bartender."

I thought about it. "I didn't know there were bartenders who were—you know, ladies."

"Oh, Fran, you're such a retard. Hey, *here* it is!" She held up the record triumphantly, moved to place it on the turntable. Soon the guitars and synthesizers and drums were pounding and Lucy jumped up, gyrating, shaking her hair wildly.

"C'mon," she called, "dance with me!"

I grinned up at her but shook my head.

"Aw, you're so *lame,* Fran!"

I watched her for a moment, then asked, "What does your dad do, Lucy?"

"Oh, we don't live with him," she said, turning away, shaking her shoulders with the beat. "I haven't seen him in a long time."

I looked at her. Halfway through the song she collapsed onto her bed, breathing hard, and picked up one of her stuffed animals, a dog. "This one's name is Big Sam," she said. "He's one of my favorites." She kissed it several times and then tossed it to me.

"He's nice," I said honestly, stroking him.

"And this is Moochie-Mooch," she said, grabbing another one. "She's temperamental. And here's Boo-Boo and Rag-Bag and Gilbert and Uncle Grumpus…" She tossed each one at me, the soft animals bouncing off my shoulders and head. I giggled.

"Where did you get them all?"

"My mom, mostly," she said. "Some of them I get out of dumpsters and garbage cans in town."

"Ewww!"

"Hey, you can get nice things in dumpsters sometimes. That's why I look in 'em. Anyway, I wash 'em in the washing machine, you know. I'm not *dirty*."

In truth, the animals were clean. "Do you have names for

all of them?" I asked.

"Every single one," she acknowledged. "And I love 'em *all.* I love *this* one," she said, hurling it at me, "and *this* one, and *this* one…!"

I shrieked and began throwing them back at her. We laughed hysterically, pelting each other with the little fuzzy animals until one careened off Lucy's shoulder, bounced against the wall, and hit the arm of the record player, creating a terrible scratching sound and stopping the song.

She looked at it, her face deadly serious, then looked at me, her eyes narrow. For a moment I couldn't breathe.

"You ruined it," she said. "You ruined my *record.*"

My heart beat wildly. "I—I didn't mean to, Lucy, it just— it just bounced wrong—"

"*You ruined my record!*" she cried, leaping at me suddenly, throwing stuffed animal after stuffed animal in my direction. She jumped on me, trying to pin my wrists, and we wrestled across the floor. I was terrified until I realized that she was laughing. Then I laughed too. We both did, hysterically, breathlessly.

Finally we parted, giggles slowly subsiding within each of us.

"That was funny," she said.

"Yeah."

"You were scared," she said, looking over at me, "weren't you?"

"I wasn't scared."

"Yeah, you were. I bet you pooped your panties."

"I didn't poop my panties, Lucy."

"*Panty pooper!*" The phrase sent us off on another torrent of shrieking laughter.

We heard a car in the driveway then, and Lucy sprang up. "My mom," she explained. "She's cool. C'mon."

I followed her out into the main room, where Ms. Sparrow was just opening the front door. She was an attractive woman with black hair, long and perfectly straight, parted in the middle, as was fashionable then. Big sunglasses hid her eyes. She wore cowboy boots, blue jeans, and a denim jacket with fringes on it like those I associated with country-western singers.

"Mom!" Lucy cried, wrapping her arms around the woman and grinning.

"Hi, Punk!" Ms. Sparrow said, smiling. "How was school today?"

"It sucked."

"Yeah, well, what else is new?" She moved into the room, dropping her car keys on the table. Just then she noticed me. She pulled off her sunglasses, revealing big silver-gray eyes that immediately reminded me of Lucy's. "Hi there," she said tentatively.

"Mom, this is Franny-Fran," Lucy informed her, skipping over to me and wrapping her arm around my neck.

I giggled again, slipped out of her grasp. "My name is Frances," I said.

"Well, hello, Frances," Ms. Sparrow said. "You're from across the street, aren't you?"

I nodded.

"You've got such a pretty smile," she said. "Look at those dimples. Jeez, Punk, don't tell me you've made a *friend*," she said teasingly to her daughter, crossing into the living room and dropping onto the sofa, pulling off her boots. "Lucy hates all the girls in that school. Can't say I blame her."

"They're *bitches*!" Lucy cried mincingly, in a startlingly perfect impersonation of me.

"Well, I don't know about *bitches*," her mom said. "But their parents have sure got some rods stuck up their asses. So what's for dinner, Frances? What have you made for us?"

I giggled. "I didn't make dinner."

"No? Goddamn it. And here I was, really hoping. Lucy, what's in the fridge?"

But Lucy didn't even have to look. "*Totino's Pizza,*" she whispered, her eyes bright.

"Oh my God," Ms. Sparrow laughed. "Frozen pizza again?"

"It's *good*!" Lucy cried.

She sighed. "I'm a bad mother. Okay. Totino's it is. Frances, are you staying with us for dinner?"

I looked at them. Ms. Sparrow had splayed herself out on the sofa, while Lucy had dropped down to the chair beside her. Lucy began methodically massaging her mother's bare feet, which were atop the arm rest.

"Mom's feet hurt sometimes after work," Lucy explained.

I stood there, curiously moved at what I saw. I couldn't imagine touching my own mother's feet, let alone those of Aunt Louise.

"I—I have to check," I said. "May I use your phone?"

"In the kitchen," Ms. Sparrow smiled, pointing with her thumb.

I ran into the kitchen, picked up the phone, dialed the number. I was sure they would say no, so when Louise picked up I simply said in a rush, "*Hi it's Frances I'm having dinner at the Sparrows' across the street okay bye!*" and hung up.

"It's okay with them," I said calmly, as I stepped back into the living room.

The dinner, pizza with various items from the refrigerator thrown on top—cheese slices, onion, strips of bologna—was delicious. What's more, it was consumed in an atmosphere of celebration: we all sat in the living room, laughing uproariously, eating off paper plates ("At least we don't have to clean them," Ms. Sparrow said with a wink) and drinking soda out of Dixie cups while the TV played *Hollywood Squares*. This was so different from the somber, tasteless dinners across the street as to seem to belong to another world. In my real home, of course, hundreds of miles away, Alba would eat with me while my parents…but I didn't want to think about that here, in this delightful company.

"Thank you, Ms. Sparrow," I said as I finished the last of my pizza.

"Oh, call me Mush," she said. "Everybody does."

"Mush?"

"Her name's Michelle," Lucy explained, stuffing pizza into her mouth.

"Oh…Okay." I could hardly imagine calling an adult just by her first name—even with my relatives across the street I always carefully preceded their names with the title *Aunt* or *Uncle*—let alone calling a grown-up a name like "Mush."

"Well," she said finally, "this has been lovely, but I've got to get back."

"You're going back to work?" I asked, surprised. It was nearly eight o'clock; *Hollywood Squares* was finishing up with a few final witticisms from Wayland Flowers and Madam.

"Split shift," she said, sighing.

"My mom works a lot," Lucy added.

Soon enough Ms. Sparrow *(Mush,* I corrected myself) had slipped on her boots again, run a brush through her hair, and kissed Lucy goodnight. "I'll be back, Punk," she said, "around two. Lock the door behind me. Okay?"

"'Kay." Lucy saw her mother to the door, accepted a kiss on the top of her head.

"Goodnight, Frances," the woman said. "Be seeing you.

Nice to meet you."

I nodded, smiling. "Thank you again."

Once the door was closed and her car had pulled away I looked at Lucy again.

"Lucy," I said, "are we really alone here?"

She shrugged, looked at me with annoyance. "Sure," she said. "What's the big deal? My mom does it all the time. She has to. She's gotta work."

"I—" The idea was sad, somehow, yet thrilling too. I was certain that Frank and Louise wouldn't approve of my staying alone with a girl my age well into the night, but I wasn't about to check.

"What do you want to do?" I asked. "Watch TV?"

"Nah, TV's pretty boring," she said, switching it off. "I mean, I like some shows. *Welcome Back, Kotter* is good. And *Starsky and Hutch.*"

"I like *Little House on the Prairie*," I said, realizing as soon as it came out of my mouth that it was a mistake.

She looked at me and laughed, her big throaty bark. "Franny, you are such a *spaz*!" But she didn't mock me beyond that; instead she grabbed my hand and pulled me back into her bedroom again. "C'mere," she said. "We'll play something *good*."

I thought that perhaps she was going to bring out a board game, but to my surprise she turned on her radio. She adjusted the station and after a moment I heard the sound of a creaking door, followed by music that sounded like it was from a scary movie. Lucy jumped to the lights and switched them off. The dull greenish glow of the radio dial provided the sole illumination in the room.

"Sit on the bed!" she whispered, as she leapt onto it herself.

I did. On the radio a man began to speak: he bade us to

come in and welcomed us.

"What is this, Lucy?" I whispered.

"Shhh!"

The man was talking about fearful things that happen in small towns. After that he said the title of *our mystery drama,* then read some credits and said that he would be back shortly with Act One. Commercials came on.

"Is this a story?" I asked.

"It's the *Mystery Theater*," she said, hugging a pillow to her belly. "I listen to it every night."

"It's like a TV show?"

She shook her head. "Better than TV," she said.

And it was. We sat there in the darkness for the next hour, listening to a story unfold about a young couple driving on some back roads who got lost in a sudden storm. They came to a creepy little town they'd never heard of and soon discovered that they couldn't leave it, no matter how they tried. The pictures played vividly in my head exactly because I had to manufacture them myself: by the end I was literally trembling with fright, pressing my shoulder against Lucy's for comfort. I didn't feel released until the host wished us *Pleasant dreams* and slowly shut his creaking door again.

"That was good!" Lucy grinned, her eyes sparkling in the darkness.

I nodded enthusiastically. But something happened then: the day, so long, so packed with emotion and event, began to catch up with me. My eyelids grew heavy. It seemed weeks since I'd stood at the bus stop that morning, seeing Lucy for the first time as she came crashing forth from this house. Soon enough I'd dropped off to sleep.

When I woke Lucy was softly snoring beside me and for a moment I was completely disoriented. The clock on Lucy's radio indicated that it was nearly midnight.

"Lucy?" I whispered, shaking her. "Lucy!"

"What?" She came awake quickly, scowled at me. "What d'you want?"

"It's midnight!"

"So?"

"I'm supposed to be home, Lucy!"

She turned over on the bed, away from me. "So go home, then."

"Lucy…! I—I'll be in trouble."

"That's your problem," she mumbled sleepily into the pillow.

"Lucy, *please.*"

She looked at me again. "What's the trouble? Just go home, Fran."

"I—" I couldn't say it.

"What?"

"Lucy, I'm…I'm afraid of the dark."

"What do you mean, you're afraid of the dark? It's dark now. Are you afraid?"

"No. Because you're with me."

"You just live across the *street,* Fran."

My breath came fast as I thought about it. "I can't—I can't go out there."

"Why not?"

"I—Please, Lucy."

"Please what?"

I swallowed. "Would you walk with me? To my house?"

"Aw, crap, Fran. You're stupid."

"I know I am."

"I mean it. You're really a spaz."

"I know."

She sighed, stretched, pushed her mop of hair out of her eyes. "All right, fine," she said at last, and pushed herself off the bed.

We made it out the door and across her rutted and pitted front yard. Everything looked different at this hour: giant shapes and shades, everything looming black and gray everywhere. I could see that lights were still on in my aunt and uncle's house, but that only seemed to make the house look evil somehow, as if it had glowing, malevolent eyes.

"I'm sorry I'm a spaz," I whispered, as we crossed the silent street.

By then she'd awakened completely and recovered some of herself. "Aw, it's okay," she said, punching me gently on the arm. "Anyway, we can't have you being a panty-pooper again."

I giggled. "I'm not a panty-pooper!"

"I'll bet you're pooping in 'em right now. I think can smell it."

"You're *gross!*" I laughed, shoving her playfully.

She saw me to my front door and we said goodnight. I watched her move back across the street, hands in her pockets.

When I opened the door it was simultaneously a relief and a new source of dread. Aunt Louise was sitting in the living room, a drink in her hand, an old movie playing softly on the television. A single lamp was on; otherwise the room was dark.

"Do you know what time it is, Frances?"

Aunt Louise wasn't an attractive woman. Her hair was a washed-out ash-white, her skin sagged around her jaws, and there were black bags under her eyes. She was heavyset and tended to wear loose dresses to try to cover the fact; they only succeeded, however, in making her look as if she wore gunny sacks. Her voice was cigarette-raspy and as far as I could see she did nothing all day other than watch TV. I hated her.

"I'm sorry, Aunt Louise," I said. "We fell asleep."

"Oh, crap."

"It's the truth," I said quietly, my hands clasped demurely before me. I could feel my usual self taking over again: no more hilarious laughter, no more throwing toys, no more excited whisperings in the dark. Just Frances again, shy, dull, obedient Frances, of no possible interest to anybody. "We really did," I insisted. "We were listening to the radio and we fell asleep."

"Don't ever stay out that late again, Frances. We're responsible for you, you know."

"I know. I'm sorry. Really."

"I think," she said, taking a drag on her cigarette and studying me with her sharp bird-like eyes, "you could do better for a friend than that girl, too."

"I like her, Aunt Frances."

"Mm. Good-for-nothing butch tomboy is what she is. Those people are slobs, Frances. Look at their front yard."

"I like her."

"Well, we'll talk about it later. Go to bed."

Without meeting her eyes I turned and moved toward my room. Once there I used the bathroom, took off my clothes, placed them with the dirty laundry, and slipped into my perfectly-ironed nightgown. Then I got into bed and lay there, my eyes wide in the darkness. My Donald Duck nightlight helped dispel some of my fear, but I felt suddenly like a prisoner. I could make my own room the way I wanted it, but couldn't control anything else. I didn't want to be here, I wanted to be home…But then I realized suddenly that I didn't want that, either…I wanted my mom to be well, I wanted my dad to…I wanted…

I wanted to be at the Sparrows'. That was what I wanted. I wanted to be with Lucy.

I lay there, a lonely ache deep in my stomach. I felt like

crying, but I didn't. Instead I thought about this house, Uncle Frank, my Aunt Louise, my stupid, broken-up life.

"She didn't even ask me how my day was at school," I whispered, to no one.

—Five—

MUMFORD IS THIRTY-FIVE miles north of Quiet along the Pacific Coast Highway, a famous drive with steep rock cliffs jutting down to the ocean on one side and endless pine forests on the other. Lovely small towns with quaint old inns and gift shops pass by the traveler's window; fishing boats crawl slowly through the waters. The road can be treacherous, with surprising serpentine curves and drops. It's easy to picture one's car careening off a sheer rock face, bouncing over the safety rail, and sailing hundreds of feet down into the ocean.

Mumford itself is tiny, nondescript. It's dwarfed, certainly, by its larger neighbors up the road—Big Sur, Monterey. There are only a few streets in the whole town and it was easy for me, following the driving directions I'd located online, to find what I was looking for. Within minutes of passing the *Welcome to Mumford* sign I was pulling up in front of the house I sought: a Victorian-era seaside cottage, lavender and navy blue, beautifully restored, with a small but flawlessly smooth lawn in front of it.

Ocean View Bed & Breakfast.

As I got out the smell of the cool salt air hit me bracingly. I blinked, looked up and down the road. There was no one. I heard only the sea.

I stepped up the walkway to the front door and pushed the doorbell, trying to slow my breathing as I waited. I'd been perfectly calm during the drive but now that I was here, actually here, my breath came fast and I felt my heart fluttering in my

52 ~ Christopher Conlon

chest. It couldn't be, I thought; I had the wrong house, I was in the wrong place, I should just turn and leave.

When the door opened I took a step back. Through the screen door a handsome woman in her sixties wearing tan slacks and blouse and a good deal of jewelry looked at me through big eyeglasses.

"Yes?" she said pleasantly.

For a moment I couldn't speak.

She cocked her head. Her upswept hair was pure white, defiantly undyed. "Do you have a reservation?" she asked.

"Hi, Ms. Sparrow," I managed to say, finally.

"Hello," she said, still smiling, but her face quizzical. "Do you…?" She didn't finish the thought.

"You used to tell me…" I swallowed. "You used to tell me to call you Mush. But I never could."

"*Mush*." She scowled then, in a thoughtful way, not unfriendly. "Oh my Lord, that goes back…how many years?"

"Thirty," I answered, without hesitation.

She looked at me again. Through the screen she appeared ghostlike, unreal.

"I'm Frances," I said at last.

I could see it didn't register with her.

"Frances. Frances Pastan…Lucy's friend."

There are moments which seem to miraculously stretch in time. To expand. It felt as if my entire life were on display, as if I were being judged, as if nothing had mattered for decades but this, that this woman should acknowledge me, recognize me, know me. I watched her studying me for what seemed a very long while, but which couldn't have been more than a second or two. "Frances," she said uncertainly.

I cleared my throat. "Franny-Fran."

Her mouth opened.

"*Frances*," she said finally, exhaling hugely. "Oh my Lord,

Frances!" She pushed the door open and wrapped me in an enormous bear hug. "I can't believe it," she said. "Oh my Lord, oh my Lord, Frances, I can't believe it!"

I couldn't speak. My throat was clogged with something thick and sour. I just shut my eyes, hugged her tightly, felt her warm arms around me. Finally we backed away and looked at each other, Ms. Sparrow's eyes full of tears. She laughed as she wiped them away.

"What are you…? How did you find me?" she asked.

I shrugged. "The Internet. It wasn't hard. I typed in your name and your B & B came up right away. I had no idea you were still—"

"Alive?"

I laughed. "I was going to say 'in the area.'"

"Well, sometimes *I'm* surprised that I'm still alive, you know?"

We laughed together. My anxiety seemed to melt away as I stood there. She was a striking woman, almost magisterial with her swooping hair, her beads and bangles. And yet behind the glasses I saw, a bit faded now yet still piercing, still attractive, her familiar silver-gray eyes.

"Frances, come in, for God's sake come *in*," she said, opening the door for me.

"Am I interrupting anything? Do you have guests?"

She shook her head. "Last ones checked out this morning. Not expecting any more until tonight. Come in, come in!"

I stepped over the threshold. The interior of the house was as beautiful as the outside. Polished wood everywhere, a fireplace in the main room, comfortable old chairs: opulent but relaxing, friendly. I'd stayed in bed & breakfast inns like this from time to time. Donald and I had enjoyed them in the early years of our marriage, a thousand years ago.

"I'm just floored that you found me," she said, leading me

into the dining room. "Would you like coffee? Tea? Please sit down!"

"Coffee would be great, if you have some," I said, seating myself in a handsome oak chair. "But you don't have to bother—"

"I have some already made," she said. "I'll just be a second." She scurried through a door which appeared to lead to the kitchen. A moment later she came back out not only with two cups of coffee on a tray, but with a huge piece of cake.

"Oh my gosh," I said. "Ms. Sparrow, I'm not sure I can eat all that."

"Try. It's strawberry." She smiled as she set it before me. Placing the tray on a side table, she sat beside me.

I did. "This is delicious," I said, honestly. She smiled again. "But you know, I don't remember you as a cook."

"Back then?" She laughed. "No, I couldn't cook a thing back then. That was a long time ago."

"Yes, it was." The coffee was excellent, too.

"Good Lord, Frances, how *are* you?" she asked, patting the back of my hand.

I smiled at her, my mouth full of cake. "I'm all right," I said, swallowing. "I was in the area."

"What do you do?"

I went through the basics of my life for her: graduate school in Arizona, children's books, Donald, Jess. I admitted the divorce but didn't mention that I never saw my daughter.

"I'm sorry about that," she said, referring to Donald, "but other than that, you've made quite a success of yourself, haven't you?"

"Yes," I said. "Other than that." Other than the fact, I thought, that I drink too much, that I take antidepressants to get through the day. Other than the fact that I can only see my daughter in the presence of her father. Other than the fact that every morning I reach for someone and no one's there.

"But how about all this?" I said, gesturing vaguely around the room. "What a success you are. This is an amazing house."

She nodded. "It took a long time. It wasn't like this when we bought it, I can tell you."

"We?"

"Jack and I," she said. "My husband."

"You're married."

"Twenty-six years, yes. I never changed my name, though."

"Twenty-six years," I pondered. I hesitated to ask the obvious question, but she answered it for me.

"We have three children," she said. "Two sons and a daughter. And a grandson." She grinned.

"Really."

She told me their names and what each of her children did for a living, but the information skated past my mind. I was thinking: *Two sons. A daughter. A grandchild.*

"Frances, why didn't you call ahead?" she asked me. "I could have given you something better than yesterday's cake."

"Oh, gee, Ms. Sparrow"—I could hardly believe I'd just said *gee,* but inevitably I felt like a child next to her—"this is great. Anyway, I—well, you know."

"Hm?"

"I—" I avoided her eyes. "Well, I—I wasn't sure you'd want to see me."

She looked at me and said quietly, "Of course I want to see you, Frances. Why wouldn't I?"

"Well—"

We left it. When I finished the cake and coffee she led me on an extended tour of the house, showing off all the gorgeous restoration work, the antiques, the furnishings.

Like all people whose lives are centered on such things, she delighted in talking about how they found a certain piece or what condition a particular banister or wall or floor had been in when they'd bought the place. I didn't listen to the specifics but I loved the sound of her voice—hearing it again. It was a bit huskier than I'd remembered, but I would have known it anywhere. Lucy had sounded a lot like her, I realized, but it was hard to think of Lucy here, in this shining well-scrubbed home, with this vibrant older woman next to me. In the sitting room I saw a framed photo of the family: Ms. Sparrow, her husband, the three adult children, all smiling in suits and formal dresses. The young woman in the photo held a baby in her arms. Nowhere in the house did I see a picture of Lucy.

"You know, I wouldn't have recognized you," Ms. Sparrow said as we sat down on a comfortably overstuffed sofa in the glowing, sunlit parlor. "How old were you back then?"

"Twelve," I smiled.

"You were such a *serious* little girl," she said. "I remember you in your very formal skirts. You wore bangs. And you hardly ever looked up from the floor."

"Really?"

"Yes. You never made eye contact. You were very shy."

I certainly wasn't shy with Lucy, I thought; but with the rest of the world, that was probably true.

"And you had—troubles, yes? At home."

I nodded.

"I remember Louise and Frank," she said, looking vaguely at some spot near the ceiling. "I can see Frank mowing the lawn on Sundays in his suspenders, with a cigar hanging out of his mouth. No shirt."

I chuckled, though I didn't know why. "That was Uncle Frank, all right." What I didn't say was: They hated you. They thought you were trash.

"Do you hear from them, Frances? Are they living?"

"No, I—I don't know. I never had any communication with them after the day I left Quiet. They don't live there anymore—I just visited the house earlier today. Different people are there now. Aunt Louise and Uncle Frank are probably dead." I tried to keep from sounding as cold about it as I felt.

"And your parents?" she asked. "I seem to remember…"

"They're dead," I said, quickly closing the subject. "A long time ago."

"Oh. I'm sorry."

We were silent for a moment. The light through the chintz curtains seemed to grow a darker gold, nearly the color of brass, as we sat there in the deepening afternoon.

"I still miss her," I ventured finally.

She looked away. "Do you?"

"She was my best friend."

"Yes." She began to pick at a spot on the sofa's arm where the thread was loose.

"I hadn't thought of her in years," I admitted. "My brain just…buried it. All of it. From that time. Everything. They took me away so suddenly at the end…You know, there was a lot of chaos in my life. My parents. Foster homes. Craziness." I shook my head impatiently. "I don't even remember a lot of it. There are years and years which are just blank to me."

"I'm sure," she said quietly, listening.

"But then I had this book thing—I told you about it—in Santa Barbara, and I realized I wouldn't be all that far from Quiet. And I knew I had to come back. It's the first time I've been in California at all since I was eighteen. I had to come back and just—I don't know. See. Remember. Something."

She nodded.

"And now it's been *flooding* back," I said. "I seem to recall everything now. Things I haven't thought of in thirty years. About my parents, about Frank and Louise, that little school… about Lucy."

She was silent, picking absently at the sofa.

"I'm sorry," I said at last. "Should I leave?"

"What?" She looked at me suddenly, as if coming out of a trance. "Why on earth would I want you to leave, Frances?"

"Maybe you don't want to talk about…"

"Oh my Lord." She smiled, shook her head, patted my hand. "Sometimes there's nothing I'd *rather* talk about."

We were silent again.

"It's nice," she said, "to see someone again who knew her. There's no one, now. No one that I know, anyway. I'm the only person I know who actually remembers her. Who has memories of her."

"Well," I said, taking her hand and squeezing it softly, "you know me. Now. Again."

She smiled and nodded. She looked very old, suddenly, in the yellow light.

"But you got past it," I said, gesturing around the room. "You moved on. That's good."

"I moved on," she agreed. "But Frances, no. I never got past it."

I waited.

"You don't," she said, "get past something like that."

She looked toward the sun-filled windows.

"You still—you still think about her a lot, then," I said.

"I never stop thinking about her. In thirty years I've never stopped thinking about her. Not for one single day." She looked around the room. "I put everything away years ago," she said. "All the pictures, school assignments, the Mother's Day cards, all of it. I couldn't stand it. Neither could Jack. He said it was like living in a cemetery. This was back when we were first married. But," she said, glancing at me again, "the family's wonderful. Jack's wonderful. He understands. So do all my kids."

"They know about it?" For some reason this surprised me.

"Oh, of course," she said. "You wouldn't want to hide something like that. She's their half-sister, you know."

I nodded. The thought was strange.

"I wasn't a good mother," she said matter-of-factly. "I was too young, too inexperienced. Too immature. And I was gone too much."

"Well, you worked a lot, I remember."

"Yes, well...I was neglectful. Didn't pay attention. It came from having a child at the age I did. And I've got to live with that. Later on, after...after what happened, I realized that I had to—I had to fix my life." She smiled, sadly.

We sat silently for a moment.

"She's buried near here," she said. There was a long silence. Then she asked: "Would you like to go and visit her?"

—Six—

SOAMES ELEMENTARY WAS abuzz with talk of Lucy Sparrow's friendship with the new girl—me. None of the talk was nice. From that very first day I'd isolated myself, cut myself adrift from my new peers by becoming pals with a girl who, I increasingly came to understand, was considered beyond the pale. The other girls made fun of her behind her back (she was fat, stupid, lumpy, dirty, except that she *wasn't*), and sometimes even within her hearing. Soon enough, inevitably, I was included as well. In English class, first thing in the morning, Lucy sat two rows in front of me, while Miriam Doyle and Company sat two rows behind; as a result, I could clearly hear their *sotto voce* whispers, designed to carry both to me and to Lucy.

"Lucy's here today," one of them would say. "I mean *Lezzie*."

"Uh-huh. I'll bet she wants to kiss a *girl*."

"I'll bet she wants to kiss that *new* girl. What's her name? Bitchy-britches."

"*Frances*," one of them said mincingly.

"She looks like she lives in a concentration camp!"

Muted giggles from behind me.

"The fat girl and the skinny girl. They're like Laurel and Hardy."

"Nuh-*uh*. Laurel and Hardy were funny. They're just gross. I *hate* lezzies."

"Why doesn't Lezzie wash her face, anyway?"

"Or her hair?"

"Or her armpits?"

"Frances could wash them for her. *She's* clean."

Giggles.

My cheeks would burn with rage and humiliation at such times. I would have fantasies of whirling on them, screaming at them to *Shut up!* and knocking their pretty little heads together hard enough to cause a resounding *thwack*. Although society tends to concern itself much more with issues surrounding high school, for many girls elementary school is much worse; the judgments there are swift, severe, and final, unleavened by any concept of empathy or pity and unredeemed by the tendency boys have to hash out their differences in sports competition or fighting. If it's true that, as Sartre puts it, *L'enfer, c'est les autres*—"Hell is other people"—then it might be that, at least for some girls, Hell closely resembles the hallways and playgrounds of a typical elementary school.

Outside of class these girls were even ruder, and I quickly learned to be at Lucy's side virtually every moment. For however cruelly they teased her, the abuse had its limits, because they were also afraid of her. She was much bigger than any other girl in the school, partly because, as I soon learned, she had actually been held back one year ("Fifth grade wasn't too great," she told me), but mostly it was just how she was built. Actual fights, common among boys, were a rarity among the girls, but nobody wanted to risk tussling with Lucy Sparrow. She was not only large, but intensely *physical*: in the first days of our friendship I'd never done such running, such jumping and throwing and catching. Lucy would quickly become restless if I suggested we simply sit under a tree at lunch. She would always urge me to join her for tetherball or tennis (she wasn't that much better than I was on the tennis court, but she hit the ball *hard*). It didn't matter what we did as long as we moved— the faster the better.

Still, the bitchy behavior never stopped. Once or twice the girls happened to catch me without Lucy, and away from adult supervision: this happened one afternoon in the girls' bathroom, when I realized on walking through the door that all three of them were standing there in a huddle near the sink. The smell of a cigarette filled the room. Melissa Deaver was the first one to see me, and for a moment she said nothing, until she saw that Lucy wasn't following me in. Then all three of them moved in for the kill.

"Well, if it isn't Concentration Camp," Melissa said, brushing her gorgeous locks out of her eyes and moving toward me. I didn't realize until too late that Susan Roselli had slipped in behind me, so that when I tried to turn to leave I was blocked.

"Let me go," I said.

"What do you mean?" Miriam said. She was the one holding the cigarette. She took a long drag on it and blew the smoke in my face. "Nobody's holding you here."

"Fine."

But when I turned, I bumped into Susan again.

"I want to *go*," I insisted.

"To the toilet?" Miriam asked. "Go ahead. Leave the door open. We'll watch. I know you'll like that. You watch your lezzie friend go, don't you?"

"No."

"Don't *lie*," she said, pushing me lightly on the shoulder. "Tell us how you watch your lezzie friend pee and then you can go."

"I don't watch her pee."

"Do you lick her pussy?"

"Shut *up*," I said. They crowded in toward me, pushing me, not hard.

"You like to lick pussy, don't you, Frances?" This was

Melissa.

"Sure she does. Yum-yum." Miriam.

"Why don't you lick Miriam's pussy, Frances?" Susan said. "At least she's *pretty.*"

"*No.*"

Susan's line convulsed them in laughter, and I took their moment's inattention to burst through them and out the door. From then on, I never went to the bathroom at Soames unless Lucy was with me.

But the fact is, Lucy *was* with me almost all the time, my personal bodyguard, and so most days at Soames featured these girls only as vague background noise. The teasing we were subjected to together was relatively mild, and Lucy once turned it to our advantage when we heard them chanting across the playground, "*FRAN-ces and LEZ-zie sittin' in a tree, K-I-S-S-I-N-G!*" She studied the girls for a moment, sneered, and then grabbed me, kissed me hard full on the lips. I started to giggle uncontrollably—the sensation, not erotic in the least, was like being tickled—and when she stopped we both looked over and saw that the girls' expressions were filled with stupefied horror. We had completely silenced them.

But Lucy had other problems with school. I was always a straight-A student—the idea of receiving anything other than an A on my report card literally terrified me—but Lucy struggled with every subject. I remember watching her in Math, where we were allowed to sit next to each other, scowling in frustration for most of the period over a worksheet which I'd finished in less than ten minutes. She would pull on her hair, chew on her pencil, scuffle her feet, sigh, doodle on the paper—it was obvious that she had no idea how to do most of the work, though she tried.

I began to help her. My homework never took me long anyway, so it was easy enough for me to do. I quickly discovered in these after-school sessions that Lucy's deficiencies were severe: I could hardly believe how little she knew. She was a bright, creative, energetic person, yet she read in the slow, halting monotone of a second-grader. Her grasp of the basics of arithmetic was shaky at best. She couldn't remember the simplest historical dates. Her essays were disjointed, incoherent; even her handwriting was a wild playpen scrawl (and such a contrast to my own tight, orderly script). I found myself growing angry, not at Lucy—never, never at Lucy—but at the teachers who, I felt, had let her down, had allowed her to drift through with D's without learning anything.

But Lucy herself was complicit in this lack of learning. She would try to pull us away from schoolwork any way she could. We might be sitting in her room with her Math book before us when she would suddenly get up, giggle, and throw a stuffed animal at my head. Or she would put on a record, saying, "Come *on,* Franny-Fran, we've been doing this for *hours,*" after five or ten minutes. "Let's have some *fun!*"

It was hard to tell her, "No, Lucy, you've got to do this, the test is tomorrow," and in truth I didn't always succeed. The siren song of goofing off with my friend (*My friend!* I'd think gleefully, *I have a friend, Lucy is my friend!*) was just too strong. At times I would try to keep her indoors, at least, with the idea—usually misguided—that after a break she could return to her homework.

Once, as she finished a math problem, she looked over at me and noticed a drawing on which I'd been doodling absently with a felt tip marker: an ouroboros, a mythological creature I'd read about—a dragon devouring its own tail. I'd illustrated it as a perfect circle, adding scales along its body and sharp ripping teeth sinking into itself.

She scowled as she looked at it. "Franny-Fran," she said, "that's *good.* I mean, that's *really* good. Wow. You can draw."

I shrugged, quickly crumpling the paper, but inwardly thrilled.

"Wait," she said, grabbing my hand. "I want it. If you don't."

"Oh, Lucy, I'll draw you a better one. I can draw a lot better than this." And it was true. I could. I knew I could draw well: I'd won a prize in fifth grade for my illustrating skills. But I didn't want to tell this to Lucy, who wasn't the sort of student to win prizes for anything.

"You should be, like, an artist," she said, smoothing the paper I'd crushed, looking closely at it.

I shrugged again. "Maybe."

"Will you really draw me a picture? One just for me?"

"Sure I will."

She grinned hugely. "Nobody's ever drawn me a picture before. I mean, a real one."

Ultimately I drew many pictures for her: angels floating in the sky, sea-serpents, horses, dragons, unicorns. Whatever I thought of, whatever she wanted. She taped them to her walls, which caused me to feel an enormous pride whenever I walked into her room. *I did these,* I'd think. *I did these, and Lucy likes them.*

More often, however, when we abandoned our studies we simply ran straight outside. Sometimes we would hop across the street, hop over the back fence, and play under the huge leafy pepper tree in my aunt and uncle's backyard. It was a wonderful place for two girls to hide, the branches strong enough to climb, the ground below softly leaf-carpeted, aromatic, smelling of spicy peppercorns and damp earth. Often my Uncle Frank and Aunt Louise wouldn't even know we were there, which was just how I wanted it. Together, in the tree or resting on the ground against its trunk, I would realize that nobody in the world knew where I was at that moment: no one but Lucy: we had disappeared, vanished completely, and if anyone wanted us they would have no idea where to look. We were just gone. Sometimes we brought Cokes and cookies from the Sparrows' refrigerator; sometimes we brought Lucy's issues of *Hit Parader* and *Tiger Beat* and *Rona Barrett's Hollywood* which, I came to realize, she got mostly for the pictures: the articles were hard for her, so I would read them aloud—but softly, softly, so that no one would guess we were there.

Sometimes we would hop on her bicycle—it was a rusty old Schwinn, what was known in those days as a "boy's bike," with a seat long enough to hold both of us if I wrapped my arms around her from behind—and ride around the neighborhood. However hazardous the arrangement, I felt safe with her in those days when no one had even heard of such a thing as a bicycle helmet. Lucy would share gossip she claimed to have learned about the people inside the houses we passed: "Did you know that Mr. Hubbard humps Mrs. Fitzgerald on Thursday afternoons?" she'd say, or, "Did you know that the Tate kid isn't Mr. Tate's real son?" How she knew these things I never asked; I simply believed her, absolutely.

Yet she said things I didn't believe, too. Once as we glided past Mr. Griffin's house on Elm Street she pointed at his van parked at the curb—actually a little brown Volkswagen Bus, the kind that once was ubiquitous on American roads—and said, "See that van? I drove it."

I looked. "Mr. Griffin's given you driving lessons?"

"No, Ricky Retardo. I mean I *drove* it. Around the neighborhood. At night."

"Oh, Lucy, no you didn't." I was slightly hurt; Lucy didn't have to lie to me, not to *me*.

"Scout's honor. He leaves his keys in it all the time. I drove it around the block once. He never knew."

"Oh, Lucy."

Increasingly we took to spending not just afternoons, but evenings together. I would help her with her homework while completing my own, then run across the street for a bland dinner with Frank and Louise.

"You're spending too much time with that tomboy," Louise would say, putting down her fork and lighting one of her endless Marlboro cigarettes.

"She's my friend, Aunt Louise. And I help her with her school stuff."

She sighed sourly. "You're still getting yours done, right?"

"Straight A's," I said defiantly. "Do you want to see my Math test? Or my Social Studies quiz? They're in my room. I'll show them to you. Hundreds on both. Or I can have my teachers call you." I was completely confident; I had absolutely nothing to hide. My schoolwork was perfect.

"All right, Frances, don't get in a huff," she said. "It's just… Why can't you have nicer friends? It's embarrassing, having you over at that dump across the street all the time. People will start to think—well, they'll think bad things about you. And about us."

"Why?" I pushed my plate away. I hated tuna casserole.

"Because they're *trash,* Frances." She said it with an oddly gentle tone, obviously aware that the words would hurt me. "Plain old white trash. I wish they'd never moved in over there. At the rate they're going, they'll pull down the property values around here. That house was bad before, but it's become a wreck since they got here."

I stared at the table, my face hot. "That's not Lucy's fault."

"Well, her mother."

"Her mother works all the time. She's never home."

"Yes. That's part of what I mean."

"I don't think they have a lot of money, Aunt Louise. That's why Lucy's mother isn't home much. She's always working. She works as a bartender. I guess they don't make a lot."

"*Bartender*," Louise muttered with disgust. "Frances, there are such nice, sweet girls who go to that school. If you'd just try to make friends—"

"I *made* a friend."

There was a long pause. Uncle Frank cleared his throat.

"Can I go over there after dinner?" I asked, looking not at Louise but at Frank. "I'm helping her with her English essay."

This was not strictly true. In fact, by dinner time Lucy and I had generally finished with homework. After dinner was playtime, girl-time.

"You know, Louise," Frank said, his voice wheezy and whispery from many years of his trademark stubby cigars, "she talked to me the other day. That Sparrow woman. She said her girl's doing much better in school now, since she's known Frances."

I smiled at him, looked triumphantly toward Aunt Louise.

"Be home by nine," she said, annoyed but, for the moment, defeated.

Evenings were always grand at Lucy's house, though my aunt's observations about Lucy's mother were not really inaccurate. She was hardly ever home, and when she was she was tired and distracted—always very nice to me (I devoured many a Totino's frozen pizza there), but she struck me as a woman whose attention was always on something else, something I couldn't quite see. She spent a great deal of time on the phone, often disappearing into the bedroom to pick up the extension there and asking Lucy or me to hang up the main line in the kitchen.

Worse than that—and a fact which I kept carefully hidden from my aunt—was the fact that Ms. Sparrow brought home a lot of men, some of whom spent the night with her in her bedroom. Lucy was always morose at these times, maintaining a minimal politeness with whoever the new male in the house was, but clearly unhappy about it. I was, too: it threw off the balance of the household, having a grown-up man around in this house of females. To her credit I must say that Ms. Sparrow seemed to watch these men carefully; they interacted with Lucy very little, mostly just vanishing into her mother's bedroom within a minute or two of coming in the door. Some of them I saw several times, some only once. But it did seem to be a constant parade. Yet I liked Ms. Sparrow, very much, and couldn't find it in myself to judge her. I just wished she would be there more for Lucy.

On the other hand, with her mother usually absent, Lucy and I had the place completely to ourselves. It was exciting to be alone together, at night, utterly without adult supervision. We could play Lucy's records at any volume we wanted, dance around her room, chase and tackle each other, drink all the soda and eat all the ice cream we could stuff into ourselves; and yet in truth these bacchanalias amounted to little but best-friend girl stuff. My own favorite time was actually not when we were being loud or rowdy, but rather the moment at a little past eight each evening when we would retire to her bedroom, shut off the lights, turn on her radio, and listen to the creaking door which opened the nightly *Mystery Theater*. Sometimes we simply lay together on her bed, our heads sharing the pillow; other times she sat on the floor with her back against the bed while I, cross-legged on the mattress behind her, spread her wild blonde hair out before me in the dim green light of her radio dial and carefully, methodically smoothed her endless tangles and rats' nests with her mother's big silver-handled brush and comb. We tried it the other way—that is, Lucy brushing my hair—but mine was short, and always meticulously groomed anyway. I liked better the sensation of her hair in my hand, flowing through the brush and comb, growing silky in my palms.

It was on the weekends, though, that we were truly free. It's not an easy thing to ride pressed behind someone on a kid's bicycle, mostly because there's no real place to put one's feet, but we somehow managed it; I was small, and Lucy was very strong. She never seemed to have any difficulty pedaling the both of us, except on the steepest uphills, when I would have to step off and walk while she chided me: "Jesus, Franny-Fran, why don't you get your *own* bike? I'm doing *all* the work here." Actually, though, while I made the excuse (which was true) that Frank and Louise refused to buy me one, I didn't really want a bike of my own. Whatever the difficulties, I loved riding with Lucy, my arms wrapped around her, my body pressed against hers, my head resting on her shoulder, my face tickled by her hair.

On Saturday mornings we would jump onto the bike and rush across Riverfield Road, out of the housing tract, onto Bridgewater Avenue and over the long bridge that spanned the riverbed, finally reaching downtown Quiet. In those days the town lived up to its odd name (which I later learned was derived not from its quiet character, but rather from its founder, a farmer with the rather aristocratic name of Quincy Cuthbert Quiet II). Little was there to tempt the interests of a couple of very young girls, but we made do even without such seeming necessities as a movie theater or a proper department store. Main Street held a couple of small clothing shops, a dry cleaner's, a grocery, barber's, and a pharmacy; it was the last of these where we spent the greatest amount of time, especially on Saturday mornings when the owner, a heavyset young woman named Mrs. Marks, would stock the wire rotating rack with its *Hey Kids! Comics!* banner at the top. Few girls read comics, and in fact I didn't until I knew Lucy; I enjoyed them because she did. Mrs. Marks was nice about letting us just sit on the floor and read them without buying any; I always felt a bit guilty about it, anyway, and invariably purchased some sodas and snacks from her for us to consume as we read. "Just don't mess them up," she would say pleasantly. But of course she had nothing to worry about: I would organize the comics before we left, leaving them in a state of virtually military order and perfection, flawlessly alphabetized, pristine.

I would do much the same thing at the library, a big old gloomy-looking building which Lucy and I would also ride to on those Saturday mornings. Initially she was resistant— "What do I want to hang around a bunch of *books* for?"—but she came to like it, spending her time in the children's section while I browsed the grown-up paperback novels, paperbacks being a new thing in libraries then. Although I had only a children's library card, Mrs. Klibo would allow me one adult book at a time based on her own personal approval. I would generally choose an Agatha Christie or Sherlock Holmes to go along with my steady diet of Nancy Drew and the Hardy Boys, placing the books in a little rucksack my aunt had allowed me to buy for the purpose. Lucy never checked out anything, but she liked whatever had lots of pictures: big splashy tomes about the movies, nature books, *National Geographic.*

There was a small general clothing store on the corner of Main and Birch Street, and it was there that I allowed Lucy to talk me into wearing jeans. "C'mon, Franny-Fran," she said, "you look too *girlie.*" She helped me try on pair after pair until we found the ones that seemed to look best; then, later, I had the job of convincing my uncle (always the looser of the two with regard to the purse strings) to give me the money to buy two or three of them, which he finally did. Soon enough the little-girl dresses were put away at the back of the closet and

I wore my jeans daily. The cardigans, too, vanished, along with the dress shoes, replaced with delightfully sloppy-looking pullover sweaters and sneakers. I never changed my obsessively clean and organized ways, not really, but Lucy's makeover definitely caused me to look like a more normal twelve-year-old girl.

On the outskirts of town were two gas stations, a big shiny Enco and, across the street from it, a dirty and dilapidated Red Ball. It was the Red Ball that attracted Lucy. Its owner was Mr. Farrington, a friendly old man with a big hair-sprouting wart on his nose. He wore filthy coveralls that smelled of gasoline and motor oil and whose hands were permanently blackened from working on cars all his life. Mr. Farrington usually offered Lucy a free piece of candy from his rather meager store behind the cash register—she always took a strip of black licorice—and when she started to bring me by, I got the same offer. We would talk then, on days when he wasn't busy; he had several rickety old chairs placed near the pumps and he could often be seen there with customers or pals, telling stories of World War II, which he'd fought in, or said he had. Sometimes he took a newspaper and read it aloud, interrupting periodically to comment on "those idiots in Washington" or "those heels on the City Council." Once, as he read a story about a proposal for a tax increase, I found myself staring with fascination at the front page he held aloft before him: *Local Girl Missing,* it read. There was a photo beneath the headline: the smiling face of a high school girl.

Mr. Farrington had someone who worked for him by the name of McCoy—"Mike," as he was called by everyone. He was a tall, reedy man, about fifty, with small black eyes and a confusion of yellow and gray teeth; he had a close-cropped butch haircut and dark beard stubble perpetually sticking out from his face, and he always wore a greasy old baseball cap on his head that said *California Angels*. Mike seemed to be Mr. Farrington's all-around helper. In that time when "full service" still existed, he was sometimes out at the pumps, filling gas, checking oil, cleaning windshields; more often he was back in the garage, his legs sticking out from under some car he was repairing. Occasionally he would take customers' money at the register. His accent was odd, obviously from somewhere else; I thought of it as *country*, Lucy called it *shit-kicker*. He smiled a lot and was very nice to the two of us, especially when we happened to show up in Mr. Farrington's absence. Then he would be much more talkative than otherwise, asking us "What'cha up to?" or "How's it hangin', lovely ladies?" while also offering us the free candy, and sodas too. "What're a couple of beauties like yourselves doin' on this fine morning? Goin' to a tea party with the other lovely ladies?"

I didn't like it when he talked to us like that, but Lucy just laughed. "I've never even had tea, Mike," she said. "Iced tea, yeah. Not hot tea."

"Well, you oughtta try it," he said, grinning at her. "Put a little rum in it. Give it some kick. You like rum?"

"Never had that either," Lucy said, shaking her head and grinning. "Had beer."

"You like beer?"

She shrugged, moving her hands absently over the displays of motor oil and air filters. "It's okay," she said.

"Well, you're a little young for it," he admitted. "It's kind of a grown-up thing."

Lucy's eyes flashed annoyance. "I'm almost thirteen."

Mike McCoy laughed. It was a harsh, throaty sound. "You're almost there, then. You'll be gettin' wasted with the best of 'em."

"You bet I will."

"You come on by sometime," he said to her, glancing at

me, including me. "I'll give you a little beer. Only a little, though. Stop by my place." He lived in a tiny house some distance from town. I'd seen it; it was plain clapboard, run-down, streaked with grime, with nothing around it but dirt and weeds. It was a house, more or less, but I thought of it as a shack.

"Maybe we will, Mike," Lucy announced boldly. "We might just do that."

"You ought," he said, nodding. "Got lots of things to do there."

"Like what?"

"Got a pool table. You girls like to shoot pool?"

"Maybe. Never tried," Lucy said.

"Oh, you'll like pool, big girl like you. You'll be good at it."

She nodded. "Maybe we'll come by sometime, then."

"Yeah. The both of you. C'mon over. We'll have us some fun."

Later, as we rode back toward town, Lucy turned her head back toward me and said, "Nice guy. Kinda weird, though. Looks at me funny."

"Me too," I said. "I don't like him, Lucy."

"But pool might be fun," she said, facing the road again and pedaling harder. "And *beer*. You want to go sometime?"

"Lucy," I said, "he's not supposed to give us beer. It's illegal."

"Oh my *God*, Fran, you're such an M.R.!" She swerved the bike then, hard, which she knew would scare me. I shrieked, tightening my grip on her waist. She did it again.

"Don't call me an M.R.," I protested. "I'm not mentally retarded."

"All right, you're a dingleberry, then."

"I'm not a dingleberry either."

"Dingleberry!"

We came to a downhill. There was no traffic so she pulled into the middle of the street, picked up speed and swerved back and forth wildly.

"Lucy, cut it out!"

"Why? You afraid? You a fraidy cat?"

"No. Just cut it *out*."

"Fraidy cat, fraidy cat!"

It suddenly occurred to me that, wrapped around her from behind, I had a weapon of my own, and I goosed her, hard, in her side. She yelped, reached around to slap my arm, and lost control of the bike. We careened to the left, then to the right. The handlebars seemed to spin backwards. For a moment I was airborne. Then my palm scraped against the asphalt and my knee banged against something hard and immovable as we crashed down into the gutter and tumbled over each other.

"Jesus Christ, Fran! That was *your* stupid fault."

"No it wasn't!" I said furiously.

"You're the one that goosed me!"

"You're the one calling me *names*!" I was crying. My hand and knee hurt, but mostly I was just frightened.

"Aw, crap," she said, disgusted, brushing herself off. "Now you're gonna be a crybaby. Great."

"Shut *up,* Lucy!"

I sat up on the sidewalk then and buried my head in my arms, gave myself over to tears. I'd been disturbed by the *Local Girl Missing* headline, the photo of the girl beneath it; uncomfortable with Mike McCoy's eyes and the things he said; terrified by Lucy's dangerous bike-riding; and finally hurled into the street, my hand torn and bleeding. I'd had enough, enough of everything.

I calmed down after a while, my breath slowing, my tears subsiding to hiccoughs. I felt lost, alone, cut loose. I felt as if my life had ended right there in the gutter.

"Here."

The voice surprised me. I looked to my left and there stood Lucy, an ice cream cone in her hand. She sat, offering it to me.

I looked away, aggrieved.

"I'm sorry," she said. "You're right. I shouldn't have called you an M.R. I'm the M.R."

Our eyes met. She handed me the cone.

"You're not an M.R.," I told her quietly.

We were silent for a time.

"Where did you get this?" I asked.

She pointed behind us with her thumb. "Drug store. At least we were smart enough to crash in front of a place that sells ice cream."

"I guess that was a good idea," I said, starting to lick it. Involuntarily I smiled.

"Yeah," she said, with a little chuckle.

We sat there in the peaceful morning, sharing the ice cream cone between us, best friends again.

Quiet ended a mile or so past Soames Elementary, at the place where the land was suddenly bisected by Highway 101. At the freeway onramp was a small state-run rest stop for travelers—nothing much, just a big colorless concrete building with restrooms and vending machines alongside a big parking lot. Surrounding this was half an acre or so of grass, a few picnic tables, a handsome oak tree. It was the kind of place thousands upon thousands of travelers had stopped at over the years on their way north to San Francisco or Seattle or south to Santa Barbara, Los Angeles, San Diego—stopped at, taken a quick stretch, gone to the bathroom, perhaps grabbed a Coke or a candy bar from a machine, and then departed, the memory of the place vanishing as quickly as the image of it in their rear-view mirrors. But for Lucy and me it became a hangout. No local kids ever came here, and the lawn was well-tended, the tree good for climbing. Though only a couple of miles from our houses, it was a place set apart, a different world: we were in the freeway culture here, people rushing up and down the state to get to their exotic, unimaginable destinations. Strangers we would never see again got out of their cars, ambled around, moved on. License plates displayed mysterious dreamlike place names: Nevada, Wyoming, Connecticut, New York.

"Santa Barbara," Lucy said one Saturday, lying on her back in the grass with her arms folded behind her head, chewing on a grass stem. "Malibu. That's where I want to go. Where there's *ocean.* And Hollywood. I want to meet John Travolta. He's a fox."

I was sitting up next to her, tearing little clumps of grass out of the ground and sprinkling them across her shirt. "He's cute," I said. "I like Donny Osmond better."

"Donny *Osmond?*" She gathered the grass I'd placed on her chest and tossed it lightly into my face. "You really *are* a spaz, Franny-Fran."

"I'm sorry," I said, smiling. "I still like him better, though."

She shook her head in mock-disgust, looking toward the parking lot. "We should hitchhike with somebody over there," she said. "Let 'em take us to Malibu and those places. Seems like we'll never get out of this dump."

We stayed there for a long time, peacefully sipping sodas and watching the traffic pass by to its unknowable destinations.

I found myself looking at Lucy, noticing again the pale brown birthmark that ran from her jaw to the middle of her neck.

"Were you born with that?" I asked, pointing to it.

"What?" She looked at me, then touched the mark, ran her finger along it. "This?"

"Yes."

I was surprised that she suddenly looked uncertain of herself, even shy. "Does it show really bad?" she asked me.

"No," I said, honestly. "It's not bad at all."

"'Cuz sometimes I think I should try to cover it up with makeup. My mom and I talked about it. We even tried it a couple of times. But…I dunno. I'm not the makeup-wearing type." She looked at me again. "It doesn't look too bad, does it?"

"No, Lucy, it doesn't look bad at all. Really. But what is it? It's a birthmark, right?"

"Nah," she said. After a moment she added, "I got cut."

I studied her, looked closely at the brown line, realized she had to be telling the truth. It couldn't be a birthmark; no birthmark was shaped like that.

"It must have been…pretty bad," I said.

She shrugged. In the stillness I reached out to her neck, touched the scar gently with two fingers. I could feel her pulse.

"Does it hurt?"

"Nah. Not at all. I don't even feel it."

I ran my fingers slowly down the brown line, suddenly heartsick that anything like this could have happened to her, to *Lucy.*

"How…?" I didn't finish the question.

"Nothing," she said, abruptly sitting up. "It was just a stupid accident. Hey, I got an idea."

"What?"

"Do you want to be blood sisters?"

I thought about it. "Is that like blood brothers?"

"Yeah. Same thing."

"I don't know," I said, a bit uneasy. "It seems kind of gross. I mean, you really swap blood?"

"Sure. Have you ever done it with anybody?"

"No."

"Neither have I. I always wanted to, though."

"Really?" I brightened suddenly as I always did whenever Lucy expressed affection toward me, even indirectly. She wanted to do something she'd never done. With me!

"How do we do it?" I asked.

"With this." She brought her little billfold out of her pocket. It contained a couple of dollars and, to my amazement, a razor blade.

"Lucy, where did you get that?"

"My mom shaves her legs with 'em. I just took one."

"You have to be careful," I said. "You might cut yourself."

She looked at me, shaking her head again and chuckling. "That's the *idea,* Franny-Fran."

"Oh. Right." I was embarrassed, but only for a moment.

The blade glinted in the Saturday sunlight. "So," she said, her voice low and excited, "are you sure you want to do this?"

"Well—can't we just use a pin or a needle?"

"I'm fresh out. You got one?"

"No."

"Well, then."

I studied her for a moment, then nodded. My breath came short.

"This is serious, you know," she said. "Being blood sisters is serious."

"I know."

"I mean, it makes us sisters. Real sisters. We share the

same blood. We're bonded forever."

"I know, Lucy."

She looked closely at me. "You're sure?"

"I'm sure."

"Okay." She nodded. "We need some paper. Like toilet paper or something. For the blood."

"I have a paper napkin." I brought it out of my pocket.

"Great. Should I go first?"

I nodded.

She looked at me and nodded back, raising her left hand, palm up. She pushed the edge of the razor into the tip of her index finger, causing a tiny droplet of blood to bead onto her skin.

"Now you," she said, trying to hand me the blade. But instead I held out my hand to her.

"No, Lucy," I said. "You do it."

She nodded, smiling. I clenched my eyes shut as she took my hand and I felt a small sting, like a needle piercing my skin. When I opened my eyes I had a similar blood-bead on my finger.

"Now," she said, "we press them together."

We moved close to each other, pushed our fingers together so that the blood commingled. We stayed motionless for what seemed a long time, then slowly parted, little blood smears like Magic Marker streaks on our fingers. Lucy tore the napkin in two and we each dabbed at our wounds. Neither of us said anything; words might have broken the spell of the moment, the feeling of solemn sacrament.

After a while Lucy wiped the razor blade and put it back in the wallet. We sat there together for a long time, close enough that our arms touched, watching the tourists' cars come and go in the parking lot. The light paled and then darkened across the grass. Finally we stood and brushed ourselves off, preparing to hop onto Lucy's bike for the ride back to town.

I knew—I believe that we both did—that words like *love* and *sister* and *forever* were inadequate to the occasion, so we said nothing, then or on the ride back. At the end, when we'd reached our houses and were about to part, we didn't kiss or hug or say friendship words. We just looked at each other, astonished at what we'd done, the importance of it, the permanence.

"Well—'bye," she said finally.

"'Bye, Lucy."

—Seven—

THE GRAVEYARD WAS less than two miles from Ms. Sparrow's house, on a gentle grassy hill overlooking the town. There were few trees, making the place look—at least to my eye—a bit like a golf course. I disliked it immediately. (But who could ever really like any graveyard?) I could see the road that had brought me here far below, the traffic moving slowly by, much of it heading south, back toward where I'd come from, in a line I would soon be joining when I left here. I knew I would never return.

Ms. Sparrow had no hesitation in moving through the main gate and then following the various paths. She knew exactly where she was going.

"I come here every few weeks," she said. "Always on her birthday. And on Christmas. The kids come sometimes too. I love them so much for that."

"Why here, Ms. Sparrow? Why Mumford?"

"There's no cemetery in Quiet, you know," she said. "Or there wasn't then. Just an old church graveyard that was already full. There's one about twenty miles north of Quiet, off 101, but I didn't like it. This was the nearest decent one in the county."

I considered.

"And after that," she said, "well, I met my husband. He's lived here all his life. So I just never left…And that's okay. I needed to be near my baby."

We passed by various old monuments –angels and cherubs, very nineteenth century, though nothing was dated

83

before 1920—and came to an area where there were several nondescript rows of ground-level plaques. Again she turned unhesitatingly, hardly looking.

"What about her father?" I asked as we walked.

"I heard he went to Alaska," she said, "twenty years ago. To make his fortune—doing what, God only knows. He always had stupid ideas like that. I have no idea where he is now. He may be dead too, for all I know. I can't say that I care."

"And…" I didn't want to say it, but I had to. "And McCoy?"

"Oh, they let him out, you know."

That stopped me, literally, in my tracks. We stood in the late-afternoon sunshine. It was a beautiful day, clear, cloudless. The shadows were slowly lengthening, darkness sliding imperceptibly across the graves.

"They let him *out*?" I said, aghast.

"Oh yes," she said, bitterness creeping into her voice. "Didn't you know?"

"Ms. Sparrow, I—I didn't know anything, until I came here today. Nothing at all."

"Well, they let him out," she said. "He spent twenty-four years in that place. That mental hospital. Atascadero. And then they just…let him out."

"But he—he *murdered* three girls!"

"Yes." She nodded, looking at the ground. "We had a lawyer, of course, for the hearings. She represented all the families. She tried hard. But they let him out anyway."

"Oh my God." I shook my head, feeling sick. "Where—where is he now?"

"I don't know. We can't get any information. Privacy rights, they say."

I looked across the grave markers. "You could probably find out," I said, silently recalling what I'd begun to understand about why I'd come to Quiet, to this area. "I mean, if you wanted to hire someone—"

"We considered that." She was silent for a moment. "But we finally decided it wouldn't serve any purpose. You have to move on, you know. Never forget, but—but move on."

She turned and started to walk again. At last we came to a simple black plaque in the middle of a row of plaques indistinguishable from it. *Lucille Catherine Sparrow,* it read, in engraved letters.

Ms. Sparrow knelt down, ran her fingers slowly across the name and dates. I stayed silent, waited for her to stand, then knelt and did the same.

"Hi, Lucy," I whispered, but it felt wrong, knowing that I was talking to nothingness. Everything seemed wrong, suddenly. The flat, undistinguished plaque. The golf-course graveyard. McCoy walking under blue skies while Lucy had to stay locked in the dark forever, rotting, disintegrating to dust. It wasn't right, I knew. It wasn't *right.*

Morbid thoughts raced through my mind. How many bits had he left her in? I wondered. And putting her in the coffin all those years ago—did they try to put her together again, in as close an approximation to a human form as they could? (A Frankenstein's monster!) Or did they simply bag her remains, toss whatever was left of her into the box in a jumble, like so much trash to be dumped and forgotten? What would she look like now, after three decades? Would her flesh still cling to any part of her? Would it have dried and mummified, stretching tight across her bones? Or would bones be all that was left, the sole remaining evidence of Lucy Sparrow's passage across this dark and merciless earth?

I stood finally. I couldn't cry. What I felt was too deep, too bruising for tears. We stood there, the two of us, gazing down at the plaque.

"I don't think I ever knew her middle name," I said quietly.

Ms. Sparrow smiled slightly, not looking away from the plaque.

"It's nice," she said finally, "when the family comes. When Jack's here, and the kids. Those are nice times. They—her brothers and sister—they bring flowers. Sometimes we sit around on the lawn here. We make her part of things." She smiled again. "And then we say goodbye…and go have lunch at McDonald's."

I laughed, a little. "Really?"

She nodded. "It's a ritual we got into when the kids were still small. It wouldn't be a proper visit if it didn't end at McDonald's."

The sun dropped lower in the sky. The plaques were enveloped in darkness now. I found myself wanting to talk, to say to her: *You never knew this, Ms. Sparrow, but I saw Lucy after you did. I saw her just before she left that night and never returned. She came to my window, Ms. Sparrow. She asked me to go with her.*

But I couldn't say it. Her daughter was at rest in her mind. It would have been the height of cruelty to open the door to that final night again, to reveal that other things had happened of which, for thirty years, she'd known nothing. No.

"Well…I'd better be getting back," I said finally.

"Won't you stay?" she asked. "I have plenty of room. You're most welcome. I mean it, Frances."

"No, I…I'd better not. I'd better go."

She nodded. "I understand." And I knew that she did.

I wanted to kneel down to the plaque again, say goodbye, but it was no good; no one was there. Instead I just stared at it for a long moment, then turned. We made our way across the paths again and toward the parking lot, where our cars were waiting. She walked with me to mine and when I opened the door she put her arms around me.

"Take care of yourself, Frances," she said. "Thank you for coming to see us. Stay in touch."

"I will," I told her, knowing I wouldn't. "Thank you so much for everything."

I got in, started the engine, and pulled slowly out of the lot, looking into the rear view mirror where Ms. Sparrow stood waving to me, growing smaller and smaller until she finally disappeared.

Michael McCoy killed young girls by drilling holes in their heads. He used the power tools he kept in his basement to do this. Sears Craftsman.

He kept other things there, too; things that were only learned of later. The basement was completely outfitted as a torture chamber. There were chains mounted in the walls. There was a bed of sorts, with leather restraining straps such as one finds in the violent ward of a mental hospital, but this one had no mattress and was outfitted with a hole in the middle connecting to a pipe which led into the floor drain. There was an Inquisition-style "rack," homemade with plywood, pulleys and rope which he bought at the hardware store in Quiet. There was a band saw. An acetylene torch. Hammers, nail guns, sharpened screwdrivers. And, for cleanup afterwards, a sink, garden hose, bleach, brushes.

I sat with my whiskey sour at the bar of the hotel in Quiet, thinking about it. I'd never known much about any of this then; I was far from Quiet by the time Lucy's body was discovered, by the time they caught Mike McCoy. That entire period thirty years before was nothing now but a jumbled impression of cries, screams, tears. It was probably better that way, I realized. What I knew now came from the newspaper reports I'd read that morning and a few things Ms. Sparrow had told me.

I wondered how he'd gotten the girls to his house; Lucy might conceivably have gone quite willingly (*Where's that pool table, Mike?*). Once there, he somehow got them into his basement (*It's downstairs, lovely lady, c'mon down, I'll show you how to play*), where there was a heavy steel door which would have closed and locked behind them. A short plywood set of stairs led down to the basement itself, which was lit by two naked light bulbs dangling by wires from the ceiling.

Nothing would necessarily have looked immediately threatening to the girls. Objects like the rack and the bed would, at least for a few moments, excite only curiosity, until the dread moment when each realized that something was terribly wrong and they turned to rush back up the stairs; McCoy would have blocked them then, probably at the base of the staircase, but even if they made it to the door, it didn't matter. It locked automatically upon closing, and McCoy had the only key.

When they realized this—maybe he told them, with a little smile on his face—they might have tried to bargain with him, or threaten him with some vague consequences (parents, police), or perhaps they just began to scream. It didn't matter. The basement was effectively soundproofed, and McCoy's nearest neighbor was over a mile away.

What did he do to them?

It was a bit different with each girl, apparently. Maria Sanchez, his first, died the fastest. I thought I could picture it, his nervousness, his fear that the police would come crashing through the door at any moment, his feeling that he had to do it *now, now or never,* and so hurriedly punching her into submission (several bones in her face were broken), gagging her, slamming her down onto the torture bed, strapping her in, finishing her with the drill as quickly as he could.

With Trista Blake he had taken longer. His confidence had grown, no doubt. He'd successfully killed Maria Sanchez, after all; not only that, he had used the band saw to chop her body into chunks, then placed them into a big plastic tub and driven them to the riverbed in the middle of the night, quietly dumping them there. He'd never even been suspected; in fact, the girl's boyfriend had been seriously interrogated by the police, to the point that his parents had threatened a lawsuit against the department for harassment and brutality. It was a month before they even found Maria Sanchez's body, the pieces of it mud-covered, rotting, picked over by crows.

It was around that time he had killed Trista Blake. She had survived, apparently, several hours, as she had been repeatedly asphyxiated nearly to the point of death before he revived her each time. Parts of her body had been burned with the torch. Finally he had finished her the same way: he drilled holes in her temple, her forehead, the top of her skull, just as he had with Maria Sanchez. One of his drill bits broke inside Trista Blake's head; it was lodged in her brain, the first significant clue the police found. And yet it led to nothing; such drill bits could be bought anywhere. The investigators really were no closer to finding the culprit than they'd been before when Lucy became his third victim.

I swallowed the remainder of my drink.

"Another, please."

The bartender brought it, placed it quietly before me. I drank it more quickly than the first one; I had to blur the visions that were forming in my mind.

How hard was it to cut a human body apart?

How much blood was there?

What did it feel like to carry chopped-off arms, legs,

torsos, heads in your hands?

I shook my head, tried to stop thinking.

So long ago. Another era. Someone my daughter's age could hardly even imagine that people lived then, in an age they saw only in old film clips. No computers, no Internet, no video games, no cell phones, no text messaging, no DVDs, no CGI, nothing that made life worth living to a girl today, a girl who was now the age that we were then. All gone, that world. Gone with the bell bottoms and the LP records. Dead fashion, dead technology. Dead and gone.

And Jess, my daughter? Not dead. But gone.

Jess has decided she'd rather not see you for a while, Frances.

What do you mean, not see me? She has to see me.

You know how upset she becomes.

I don't care, Donald. I have a court-ordered right…

I'm not so sure. After this second accident.

It was a fender-bender. It was no big deal.

She was in the car, though. And you failed the Breathalyzer test.

That test was crazy. I'd had one drink. One. Drink.

But Frances, on top of the other, before, when you nearly…

Don't say it. Don't.

You have to face reality, Frances.

Reality: sitting in my ex-husband's house, he and his new wife hovering nearby, watching, while I sat humiliated across from my daughter in their living room and tried to think of something to say to her, anything at all that might interest her, while she slouched there on the sofa not making eye contact, her long hair hiding her eyes, chewing gum and blowing bubbles, flipping through magazines, never speaking to me, never acknowledging my presence. *How is school? Do you have a favorite teacher? Are you playing sports now?*

Then Jess looking toward her father and stepmother: *Is the hour up yet? Can I go?*

Remembering my own parents, the tears and recriminations, the needles, the strange people in the house in the middle of the night, it was like an endlessly recurring phantasm: they'd failed me, failed me when they herded me off to Uncle Frank and Aunt Louise in the middle of the night, failed me after I returned when police cars came with lights flashing and broke down the front door of that *upper-middle class home in one of Fresno's most beautiful neighborhoods,* as the media said later, the kind of place where *things like this just don't happen,* and yet they did, the two of them led off in handcuffs in *Fresno's biggest drug bust in a decade,* huge quantities of heroin and cocaine and marijuana in the basement, in their bedroom, in the hall closet. And Alba holding me tight in my room, saying, *Don't look, sweetheart, don't look,* though I couldn't help but see the red-and-blue flashing lights outside, hear the crashing of the door, the shouted voices. They'd failed me. Just as, now, I'd failed Jess.

Red-and-blue lights against the night, three decades later. Coming to consciousness, realizing blearily that I was behind the wheel of my car, the inflated air bag dust-odored in my face. Hearing voices around me, a knock on the door, uniformed policemen peering in. Then looking to my right, seeing Jess slumped against the passenger side window, forehead and lips bloody, front tooth split vertically to her gums, left cheek gashed and purple, but most of all, by far worst of all, her eyes closed, mouth agape, her body utterly, horrifyingly still.

Jess! Jess!

I thought of the ouroboros, the self-devouring serpent-beast I used to enjoy drawing when I was a girl. Somewhere my life had looped back into itself and I'd wound up replicating the same disasters my own parents had inflicted on me. In my own way, certainly; as a result of my childhood I'd never had anything to do with drugs, for instance, yet alcohol had proved a worthy substitute, as it had been the night I'd taken Jess to a movie and then dinner—it was the first time I'd seen her in a month, I was giddy with excitement—and ordered the first drink, just a single glass of wine, followed by a second and, almost unconsciously, the third….

I'd started drinking while I was in the various foster homes to which I was assigned after the catastrophe with my parents. Alcohol unfocused things, I found. Blurred them marvelously. Took away the harsh and dirty edges and made everything smooth and clean. I drank through high school, through college, through the early years of my marriage, keeping the weight off by fiercely devoting myself to my morning workouts at the gym. Running, cardiovascular machines, weight training, swimming. Sports whenever I could. I was known as a fitness nut. And Donald drank a good deal too—we drank together—until one day he decided that he would stop.

I never stopped.

My life kept looping back, encircling itself, eating itself. Somewhere it had all gone wrong and nothing I'd ever done had put it right. At this point I didn't know how; I didn't know what "right" was. There had been a second accident with Jess nearly a year later; minor in itself, with no injuries, it had nonetheless led to my failing a Breathalyzer test; and that was the end, of course. Donald and his wife took full custody, reducing me to brief supervised visits during which Jess read magazines and blew bubble-gum bubbles. When I thought of her now, I felt utterly, comprehensively defeated, as if I could just cry for the rest of my life and still not be done with tears.

Donald, ask her to come to the phone, please ask her.
She won't, Frances.
Just for one minute. Exactly a minute. Sixty seconds.
She won't, Frances.

I swallowed the last of the whiskey sour and got up to leave. Had my life been hopelessly off-course even when I'd lived here in Quiet? I didn't think so. No, at that point there had still been the possibility of salvation. Frank and Louise hadn't been loving, but they had provided me something like a home. I did well in school, as I always had. And there was Lucy, whom thirty years of eating my own tail had nearly obliterated from my memory. For three decades the very thought of her had been too much to contemplate. She'd vanished from me, from my mind, though of course she hadn't. Not really.

Without any conscious thought of where I was going, I wandered through the hotel lobby and out the sliding-glass front door to the parking lot. I was restless, shaking slightly, unwilling to go back to my room where, I knew, I would simply continue drinking. I'd had two whiskey sours but I knew I was all right to drive. Would I pass a Breathalyzer test if I were pulled over? Possibly not. But I wouldn't be pulled over. I would be careful.

And I was. I got into my car, switched on the headlights, eased out of the lot and onto Main Street. It was late, past eleven. Thirty years ago the town would have been dark, lifeless; now, there were places still open. A car sat in the drive-through at the Burger King, the young woman in the window handing the driver a white bag. I saw customers wandering the aisles of the video store across the street. A restaurant or two hadn't yet closed; there were diners visible in the windows. The streets were well-lit here, nearly as bright as day; how different from back then, when by this time the town would be virtually enveloped in darkness. The rest stop near the freeway was still there too, though massively built-up now; what had been an expanse of green grass was now a glittering Tourist Information building. The tall oak that had once stood there was entirely gone. I turned off before I reached the onramp, not stopping.

Instead I drove onto the street which, I thought I recalled, led to where the gas stations had been, and sure enough, where I remembered the Enco the bright lights of an Exxon soon appeared before me. Though renamed, it was much the same place as back then, bigger now, with a friendly-looking mini-mart connected to it (also open). Across the street, however, there was no evidence whatsoever of a grubby little gas station called the Red Ball. In its place stood a shining Merchant's Tire and Auto Center, closed for the night.

I pulled to the side of the road, studied the spot for a moment. The building was big, clean, and attractive. It was hard to believe that Lucy and I had ever sat there on Mr. Farrington's chairs, watching the cars go by, eating free candy with him. Harder still to think that Mike McCoy had worked there, right there, had talked to us, called us *lovely ladies.*

I drove on. Somewhere up ahead, on one of the little dirt side roads, would be the spot where Mike McCoy had lived. The house I thought of as a shack.

More of the roads were paved than had been thirty years before, and the businesses came farther out into the country, but they still trickled off eventually and left only open fields. I turned onto a side road, thinking this might be it, but after a few minutes I saw nothing that looked like his house. I backtracked, tried a different road; again nothing. It seemed very dark out here. After a time I felt my heart beginning to race. One of these roads was the right one, I knew. One of them led directly to the place where McCoy had lived, even if the house no longer existed, which it probably didn't. I was very close to where he had kept his basement, close to where he had killed the three girls, close to where Lucy had been drilled into and hacked apart. I might be driving past it even at this moment, the place, the very place.

But I couldn't find it, and after a while I became fearful

that I would get lost on these obscure back roads. Yet perhaps, I reasoned, that wouldn't be so bad. I kept driving, circling around, trying this road and that, crawling through the darkness, imagining that eventually I might come across Lucy, her ghost, standing there at the side of the road, beckoning to me, waving, calling, *C'mon, Franny-Fran. Come on out. We'll go someplace. Together!*

If she appeared, I thought, I'd go with her. This time I would.

—Eight—

DESPITE MY STELLAR grades, and Lucy's ever-improving ones (she was managing C's within weeks), the friction between my guardians and me regarding the time I was spending across the street didn't abate. Uncle Frank was neutral on the subject, as he was neutral on everything—he was willing to float me some cash occasionally, if I had my eyes on a new pair of jeans or a book or something, always leaning down to me and whispering *sotto voce*, "Don't tell your aunt, all right?" But other than that he paid little attention to me. Dealing with Frances was left to my aunt, a tired and, I think, rather bitter woman who was preoccupied with appearances. I couldn't imagine—I still can't—who on earth could possibly care if I hung out at the Sparrows' house, but Louise was convinced that the neighbors would all brand us as all "trash."

"Aunt Louise, who cares what they think?" I asked one night. I was late in coming home: Lucy and I had lost track of time, it was 11:00, and there she was in her chair with her Marlboro, demanding to know what I was doing out at all hours of the night, demanding to know what I believed the neighbors would think of my behavior. "Why would anybody pay any attention?"

"But people do, Frances. That's what you don't understand."

"It's not people," I said. "It's *you*. You just don't like them."

"You're right. I don't. But it's more than that."

The TV was on as we argued, and we both heard the word "Quiet" at the same time. We stopped speaking and looked toward the screen. The Monterey-area news anchor, Bill Bollin, was saying that a body believed to be that of Maria Sanchez, a girl who had been missing for the past several weeks from her hometown of Quiet, had been found in the riverbed north of the town. There was a report from the scene: a man with a microphone asking the local sheriff for details about the case. I recognized the sheriff, Jim Langston—Lucy and I often saw him in his uniform on the streets of Quiet; sometimes he lifted his hat to us and smiled as we rode by—and I recognized the riverbed, too. Lucy and I had wandered around in it. Maybe not in that exact spot, which was quite a distance north, but the topography all seemed familiar.

"There, you see?" Louise said triumphantly. "You see how dangerous it is to be out in the middle of the night?"

"Shh! I'm trying to listen!"

The sheriff was saying that nothing like this had ever happened in Quiet and that state authorities were coming in to help with the case. The reporter asked him if he suspected foul play and the Mr. Langston's face grew pensive, even, I thought, frightened. "Yes," he said. "From the condition of the body…Yes. Foul play. Definitely." The picture cut back to Bill Bollin, and the story was over.

"All right, then," Louise said. "No more nighttime visits with your friend. I want you in before dark."

"That's not fair."

She gestured toward the television with her cigarette. "Frances, for God's sake, you *saw* that story! It's a dangerous world out there. You don't understand."

I thought of the crashes and cries in my own home, pictured my mother with a syringe in her arm, glassy-eyed, saw my father moving toward the door, shouting *Get out of here!* as he slammed it in my face.

"I know it's a dangerous world, Aunt Louise. But Ms. Sparrow is usually there—" a bald-faced lie—"and Lucy just lives across the *street.*"

"Frances, I want you to be safe."

"No you don't!" I exploded. "You don't! You don't care one bit!"

"Stop that. Don't talk to me like that."

"I'll talk to you any way I *want* to! You're not my mother!"

"Frances…"

"*You're not my mother!*" With that I ran to my room, slammed the door shut, threw myself onto the bed, and gave myself over to tears.

Thus it was that I became a rebel.

A very timid rebel, to be sure; but a rebel nonetheless. I started to leave my dirty clothes on the floor of my room instead of picking them up, knowing it would mean that Louise would have to come get them. I left dishes and glasses around the house. I stopped organizing my closet and bureau with such obsessive focus—they were still quite tidy, in truth, and I knew Lucy would have laughed if I'd called my room sloppy; still, they weren't as they had been. More importantly, I began to let my schoolwork slide a bit. Again, the slide was very slight, but I found a grim, dirty-feeling satisfaction to see the occasional B on a quiz sheet. Even Lucy was surprised at me.

In truth, the moratorium on after-dark visits didn't have much practical effect on our relationship. I just left a little earlier each night, that's all. We still played, and danced, and horsed around; I still ate bologna-covered pizza with them when Ms. Sparrow was at home. But I had to leave before the *Mystery Theater* came on, so I got Uncle Frank to loan me an old radio of his that was sitting in the garage and I listened to it myself, in my room. It wasn't the same, of course. But at least Lucy and I could talk about the stories on the bus the next morning.

The weekends were unchanged, too. We rode everywhere, discovered strange things. One afternoon we wandered into the market down the street and found to our astonishment Mr. Cox, the bus driver, standing behind the meat counter. Lucy and I stared at each other wide-eyed, ran back out of the store before he saw us. By the time we reached the curb we were doubled over in laughter.

"Mr. Cox has another job!" I shrieked. It seemed scandalous, somehow.

"Yeah, *Dick Cox* and his *meat*!"

I don't think even we could have explained why we found this so gasp-inducingly hilarious, except that it was one of those childhood shocks: to learn that an adult in our lives was something else, something *more* than just the bus driver was a bizarre, giddy-making fact. I'd once had the feeling when I was walking and noticed Mr. and Mrs. Lowther, packages in their hands, unlocking the door to a house and stepping inside it. *A house?* I wondered. *Mr. Lowther lives in a house? With Mrs. Lowther?*

Another time, a sunny April day, Lucy had decided to root around in the garbage behind the little row of shops on Main Street. "C'mon," she said, "it's fun! I told you, I get a lot of my stuffed animals from dumpsters. You find great stuff in here!" She climbed up onto the big metal bin that squatted there. The lid was already open.

"Lucy, I'm not digging around in *garbage*!"

"Don't have a cow, Franny-Fran. I'm not gonna *dig around*

in it. I'm just gonna take a look-see." She leaned over into it, her rump in the air. "Sometimes," she said, "you can find, like, candy and stuff. I mean, still wrapped up. They throw it out when it gets old. Once I found a whole bunch of comic books. And—" She stopped then, rooted energetically for a moment, then pulled something out. "Oh, wow!" she cried.

"What? What is it?"

"Ha! You won't believe it!"

"*What?*"

She climbed back out, stood triumphantly with a rolled-up magazine in her hand. "Wouldn't *you* like to know," she said.

"What? Tell me, Lucy!"

"No!" She stuffed the magazine, cover facing her, into the front of her pants.

"Tell me! Come on!"

"No." She grinned. "C'mon, let's get out of here!" She jumped down from the dumpster, leapt on her bike. "Well, are you coming?"

I scowled, jumped on the bike. As she pulled onto the sidewalk I tried to grab at the mysterious magazine in her pants. She batted my hands away. "Cut it out," she giggled. "You'll see. When the time is right."

"Oh, I'll bet it's nothing anyway. Just an old *Tiger Beat* or *Dynamite.*"

"Oh, no it's not."

"Well," I sniffed, "I don't care."

"Liar."

"I'm not a liar."

"Liar, liar, pants on fire!"

I grabbed for the magazine again. She batted me away.

We rode out to the rest stop, where the usual assortment of travelers was coming and going. Lucy stopped the bike in front of the women's restroom and we jumped off. "C'mon in," she said.

"No, I'll wait out here. I don't have to go."

"Come *in*," she insisted, grabbing my hand and pulling me.

She checked to make sure the bathroom was empty, then pulled me into a toilet stall and locked the door behind us.

"Lucy, what are you *doing?*"

She grinned, pulling the magazine out of her pants. "Look."

It was a copy of *Playgirl.*

"Oh my God!" I whispered, awestruck.

"Told you it wasn't *Tiger Beat*," she said. She was whispering too.

I felt nervous suddenly, terrified, positive that the police would come crashing through the door at any second to arrest us, haul us off to jail. I could see my aunt and uncle having to come get me, being told that I'd been *detained* for the crime of looking at dirty pictures. I knew what *Playgirl* was—every girl did—but I'd never actually seen one.

She opened it, flipped quickly to the centerfold, and I beheld my first naked man.

"Ew," I said quietly. "Gross."

We stared at the magazine for a long moment.

"Why is he so *hairy?*" I whispered. "He looks like a gorilla."

"All grown-up men have a lot of hair, stupid. So do ladies."

"Not *that* much. And not *there.*" I pointed.

"Yeah, there."

"Really?"

"Really."

I frowned. "How do you know?"

"'Cuz I'm smart. I'm a lot older than you, Franny."

"We're both twelve."

"Yeah, but you just *turned* twelve. I'm almost thirteen."

We flipped furtively through the pictures.

"Do you think," Lucy said, "that Art Green's is like that?" Art Green was a boy in our class.

"No. I don't think anybody I know is like *that*."

She looked at me, giggling. "The teachers are. Mr. Lowther is."

"No he's not!"

"He's a grown-up man, isn't he? And Mr. Blatt. And"— she giggled again—"Mr. *Dick Cox*."

We shrieked with laughter, with embarrassment, a giddy criminal high. The thrill of standing in a public toilet stall looking at pictures of nude men sent electric jolts through me, made me tingle and sweat.

But suddenly the bathroom was filled with noise: a bunch of little girls had burst in. We heard the voice of their teacher or whoever it was telling them to *line up, wait your turn,* and then one little girl's voice saying, *There are two people in that one!*

Lucy and I gasped, dropping the magazine. We stood frozen. My heart was smashing against my chest.

"Come on," Lucy whispered.

"No, we can't go out there!"

"Yes we can. Don't say a word. Don't look. Just go straight out."

"*Lucy…*"

But she unlocked the door, opened it, and walked unflinchingly across the length of the bathroom. I followed sheepishly behind her, staring at the gleaming tile floor. When we reached the outdoors, we scrambled to her bike.

"Hey!" a little blonde girl called, standing in the doorway.

"You forgot something!"

"Forgot what?" Lucy said. Even she seemed a little scared.

"You forgot to wash your *hands!*"

We both laughed then, and rode away as quickly as Lucy could pedal.

We realized only later that we'd forgotten something else, too: we'd left the magazine on the floor of the stall.

Later that afternoon we sat under the pepper tree in the backyard, thumbing listlessly through an issue of *Hit Parader.*

"I wish we hadn't forgotten it," Lucy said, tossing pebbles against the trunk of the tree.

"I'm glad we did," I said. "It was disgusting."

She looked at me and chuckled, shaking her head. "Fran, you're a spaz."

"I know."

"You're gonna *marry* one of 'em someday, you know."

"No I'm not." I shook my head vehemently.

"What, you're gonna stay alone all your life? Become a nun or something?"

"Maybe. But I'm not going to marry somebody like *that.*"

"You will," Lucy said confidently. "You'll have kids, too, I bet."

"I'm never having kids. I *hate* kids."

I found an article in the magazine about Linda Ronstadt and read part of it aloud, but my mind wasn't on it. Neither was Lucy's. After a while I stopped.

"What'll you do, then?" she asked me.

I thought about it, but I couldn't imagine a thing: the future just seemed to be filled with empty space, cold, desolate.

There was no way I could ever be a grown-up.

"I don't know," I said. "What about you?"

"I could get married," she said, tilting her head thoughtfully. "I think I could. Someday."

"To a *man?*"

She laughed. "Well, who do you think I'd marry?"

"And—" My face burned as I thought of it. "And—and you'd have *sex* with him?"

"Sure," she said casually. "Why not? I bet it's not that bad. I mean, people do it, don't they?"

"Perverted people, maybe!"

"Franny…all the grown-ups we know have *sex*."

"No they don't."

"Sure they do. Look at Mr. and Mrs. Lowther. They have two kids—where do you think they came from, the stork? Mrs. Petrie is married too. And I even heard *Dick Cox* say something about his wife once."

"Don't, Lucy. It's too…*weird* to think about."

But she was enjoying needling me. "Imagine," she said in hushed, teasing tones. "Imagine Mr. Lowther naked, with a hard-on. Big as a cucumber and poking out."

"Don't—"

"And Mrs. Lowther spreading her legs open and him sticking it into her…"

"Don't!"

"…and humping away on top of her, squirting *come* into her *pussy* and making *babies*…"

"*Don't!*" I covered my ears.

She laughed suddenly, her usual big bark, and threw a handful of pepper leaves at me.

"Spaz," she said, without malice, smiling.

"Please stop talking about gross things," I said, seriously.

Her face softened a little. "Oh, okay. Forget it. Hey," she

said, "you don't even know from gross, anyway. Wait 'till you get your period."

I looked at her. "Have you gotten yours?"

She nodded. "Since last winter."

"What's it like?"

She glanced at me and, I could see, made a decision to spare me the gruesome details. "It hurts," she said, "but it's not that bad."

"You get it every month?"

She nodded. "It's no fun. But don't worry about it, Franny-Fran. There's nothing you can do about it, anyway. It just comes. You'll be okay."

I was aware that she was sparing my feelings. "I hope I never get it," I said, but even as the words came from my mouth I knew they weren't entirely true. On one level I *did* hope I'd get it. It would bring me closer to Lucy, make me a little more like her, give us one more thing to share. But it also seemed the passageway into another world, a dark, frightening one from which there was no return. Lucy got her *period,* I thought. That means she could have a *baby.*

I felt lonely then, as the sun dropped behind the house and we were enveloped in shadows. Lucy inhabited a different world from mine. I didn't like that thought. I didn't like it at all. I started to cry softly.

"Franny-Fran, what's wrong?"

"Just—can we please talk about something else?" I was embarrassed, but I couldn't seem to stop. "I don't want to talk about—about naked men and—and—and periods—and stuff…"

"Franny, I'm sorry. I didn't mean to get you worked up." I felt her hand on mine and I grabbed onto it, held it tight. "C'mon," she said gently, cajolingly, "cut it out. You cry too much, Franny. Why are you crying?"

"I don't know."

But I did. All the talk of grown-up things had made Lucy seem distant, beyond me. She was going places I wasn't ready to go, not yet.

"Lucy?" I said. "Please don't…don't go away. From me."

She looked at me, puzzled at my sudden emotion. Then she tousled my hair playfully. "What are you talking about, Franny-Fran? I'm not going anywhere. You're my sister, remember? Blood sisters."

There was surprisingly little talk of the Maria Sanchez case in Quiet, but it may only have been that adults were circumspect in what they said around children. Too, there was an assumption on the part of many people, even law enforcement, that this was something personal: a family member, a boyfriend whose mind had gone haywire. Tragic, horrifying, but most likely nothing of any further importance. Anyway, Maria Sanchez was a Mexican; her mother worked as a cook and her father as a gardener. That shouldn't have made a difference but, I understand now, it did. When the victim's boyfriend was arrested, that seemed to slam the matter shut forever.

Everything changed with the Trista Blake case. Maria Sanchez's boyfriend was in custody when Trista Blake's body was found in the same riverbed, a mile north of the first location. Her body, what remained of it, was fresh; she'd been killed within twenty-four to forty-eight hours of the discovery of her dismembered corpse. Trista Blake and Maria Sanchez had gone to the same high school, but they inhabited different worlds. Maria Sanchez had been quiet, unobtrusive, her English less than fluent; she was chubby, not notably attractive; she had mostly hung out with the handful of other

Hispanic students in the school. Trista Blake, on the other hand, was the daughter of the man who owned the grocery store downtown; she was a junior varsity cheerleader, she was in drama club, she was on the staff of the school newspaper. She was pretty, a willowy blonde with feathered hair. She was one of the popular kids. And now she was dead.

I wasn't much aware of these events then; I wasn't interested in TV news, and the headlines in the paper caused me a momentary sinking sensation, no more. To be *killed,* I remember thinking. To be *murdered.* But it was impossible to visualize; I knew no details of the cases, only that girls I'd never met, never even heard of, had disappeared and then their bodies had been found in the riverbed. There was an unreal quality to it, as if this were a movie, not life. It wasn't something I thought a lot about.

But the impact in the town was immediate. Lucy and I rode across the bridge one afternoon, staring with fascination at the numerous police cars and dozens of uniformed men a hundred feet below. And suddenly policemen seemed to be everywhere on the streets of Quiet, not talking, not interacting with people, just strolling the sidewalks, cruising Main Street in their vehicles. It created an odd, uneasy atmosphere.

Aunt Louise was nervous, pensive. "When you come home," she told me at dinner one night, "come straight in. Don't go to your friend's house. I want you home."

"Why?" The situation was still unreal to me. "I'm just as safe at Lucy's house. Nothing's going to happen, Aunt Louise."

"You're *not* as safe at Lucy's house. That woman, her mother, is never home."

"Well, then, let Lucy come here," I said.

And, to my surprise, that was what happened. Aunt Louise couldn't in good conscience argue that a child, even one with a mother she despised, should be left alone in a house by herself at night, not in these days of girls turning up dead in riverbeds. And so Lucy began coming to our house.

Those were some of the finest times we had together, even though we didn't have the run of the place the way we did across the street. We couldn't charge through the hallway, toss Nerf balls at each other, gorge ourselves on ice cream. These occasions were quieter; it was a quiet house, after all. Even funereal. Lucy and I stayed in my room, chatting, doing homework, drawing, and listening with the lights off to the nightly *Mystery Theater* (together! together again! I thought joyfully), my own brushes now making their way through Lucy's ever-tangled hair, the two of us enraptured by the suspense stories we heard and then drowsy afterward.

Once we were inspired by a story Mrs. Petrie had read to us in class. Somewhere in the Midwest a company had been excavating a former school site, preparing to build a shopping mall there, when they discovered a metal box under the ground. On opening it they found that it was a time capsule. Placed there as a class project during World War II, it was filled with relics of thirty years before: photos of the students in the class, contemporary news magazines, a baseball glove, a food rationing coupon, a Captain Midnight secret decoder ring, and much more ephemera from that lost era. With all of it was a letter from the class that began: *Hello, People of the Future. We are burying this time capsule on March 3, in the Year of Our Lord 1943.* Newspaper writers had made much of the find, looking up students at the school from three decades before who had memories of the project (and of the school, which had closed twenty-five years earlier). Mrs. Petrie suggested that Soames Elementary should do something similar, and for a few days there was considerable excitement about the idea, but for some reason it never materialized.

Lucy and I didn't forget about it, however. Alone in my bedroom at night we decided to make our own time capsule, fill it with the things that mattered to us, and bury it somewhere—maybe in the back yard, maybe at the school.

"But what'll go in it?" I asked.

"Oh, stuff," she said, considering. "How about my Math book?"

I smiled. "You can't do that."

"Oh, well. Um…Some of your drawings, Fran. The ones of the dragon eating its own tail. And the ones of angels that you draw. We should show the people of the future what *real* talent is."

"Lucy, I'm not that good."

"Oh, and some *Tiger Beat*s. Ones with good pictures of John Travolta."

"I don't want to make the time capsule for just anybody, though, like that school did." I had an idea. "We should make it for us. Just for us, for us to find, in the future."

"You mean, like, when we're old?"

"Sure. We'll agree to come back to where we buried it twenty or thirty years from now. We'll set a date. We'll go together and dig it up."

"Yeah, that's cool. But we can't tell anybody."

"No, definitely not."

And for weeks we found ourselves thinking about items that could go into the capsule and things that had to stay out. We decided to keep it small, thus making it easy to bury, but also canceling the possibility of full-sized magazines and things like that. (Lucy did, however, insist on clipping some individual photos of John Travolta for inclusion.) We'd use one of my aunt's Mason jars, tightly closed, reinforced with my uncle's electrician's tape, and then placed into a strong cardboard box with lots of cushioning. The digging wouldn't be a problem; my uncle had a couple of shovels. We considered and rejected dozens of potential locations for the burial of the thing.

In the meantime Ms. Sparrow and my aunt and uncle came to some sort of arrangement regarding pickup times for Lucy. Sometimes she would come knocking at our door, other times Uncle Frank would walk Lucy over to her house at night, always with me along. And at times, when Ms. Sparrow was there, we would still spend evenings together at Lucy's. I was amazed that my aunt was working together with Ms. Sparrow on all this, but the fear of what the TV news was now calling the *Riverbed Killer* was strong.

But Lucy was becoming restless during our nightly visits, and once, when we were at her house and her mother had gone to bed, she suggested something truly daring.

"Hey Franny-Fran," she whispered, though we were in her room and far from any possibility of her mother hearing. The room was dark. The *Mystery Theater* had concluded a long time before, but it wasn't a school night, so I was allowed to stay later—until midnight. We had just remained together on the bed after the show had finished, listened to the news, listened to music, drowsing. It was late. "Let's go outside. I wanna show you something."

"Outside? We're not allowed to go outside, Lucy."

"So what? Are you a fraidy cat?"

"No. But my uncle will pick me up in an hour."

"We won't be gone an hour. We'll be back in plenty of time."

"Lucy, no. We should stay here. What if he finds out? What if your mom does?"

She made a sour face. "When Mom's with one of her boyfriends in the bedroom she doesn't come out until morning," she said. "And your uncle never picks you up early.

Come on."

"What do you want to do? Can't we just do it tomorrow?"

"Uh-uh. This is something secret."

"Lucy...I don't know. We better not."

"Fraidy cat."

"I'm not. Stop calling me that. Anyway, how would we get out? Your mom would hear the front door."

"Ha." Lucy leapt up in the darkness and moved to her bedroom window, slid it open. The night air was cool. She reached to the window screen and in one smooth, silent motion, pulled it out.

"Lucy! You broke it!"

"I didn't break it, Spazzy-Spaz. It fits right back in. I've done this before."

I got up, stood with her next to the now gaping window, the night breeze on my face.

"You know I'm scared of the dark, Lucy."

"But you're not scared when I'm there, right?"

"Yeah...I guess," I said doubtfully. "But...what if we— you know, get separated or something?"

"We won't," she said, taking my hand. "I'll stick by you every second. I swear. Really. I'm sincere."

"Lucy," I said, trying to turn away, "I don't know...Why don't we just..."

"Come *on*, Franny!"

I looked at her in the darkness. Her silvery eyes shone brightly, waiting. Finally I nodded.

She climbed out first—an easy thing, the window was low—and then stood waiting for me, her arms up to take my hands as I clambered through. In a moment we were outside, in her tiny backyard, blackness everywhere around us.

"Come on!" she said, excited. Holding my hand, she led

the way, running around the corner of the house and onto the sidewalk.

"Where are we going?"

"You'll see!"

We ran for maybe a block. She led us straight to Mr. Griffin's house and his brown VW Bus at the curb.

"Lucy, *no!*" I gasped, remembering her story.

"Yeah! C'mon!"

"What if he *hears* us?"

"He's not home, you dip. Look. His car's gone."

"But—Lucy—"

The street was silent. There was no traffic, no movement at all. We might as well have been drifting in outer space.

"C'mon. Get in. You didn't believe me before. But I'll prove it. I *have* driven this van."

"I—Lucy, I believe you. I really do. Now let's—"

But she turned away, opened the driver's side door, which was indeed unlocked. And to my horror I could see the keys sitting in the ignition. She hopped onto the seat.

"C'mon," she said. "Get in the other side."

"Lucy…Lucy, you said you wouldn't leave me alone in the dark…"

"And I *won't.* Just get *in.*"

Sighing, trembling, I ran around to the other side, climbed into the van. We closed the doors softly. The interior of the vehicle had been completely gutted; there was little inside it at all. A few blankets, a thin and torn carpet on the floor. Mr. Griffin used it to collect the bureaus and beds and tables he sold in his second-hand furniture store.

"Watch," she said.

She turned the key and the engine rumbled into life. It sounded like a bomb blast to me, like a sound that would send everyone out of their homes into the street to see what was happening. I looked around frantically, terrified.

But suddenly we were moving. Lucy pushed down the clutch and eased the van into gear and we were actually in motion, sliding slowly along the street just like any other car. She switched on the lights then. They looked like luminous ghosts in front of us. Lucy looked over at me and laughed.

"Stop being so *scared,* Franny! I told you, I know how to do this! My mom let me drive her car around a parking lot a couple of times."

Just as she said it, however, a pair of headlights appeared, coming toward us. I sank down in my seat, clenched my eyes shut, tried to shrink, tried to disappear. I realized that I was about to pee in my pants and I tensed my legs, pushed them together tight, willed myself not to do it.

"Lucy—oh my God, Lucy—"

I was positive that it would be a police car, that its lights would suddenly flash and its siren blare, but no: it was just another car, after all. It passed us without incident.

Somehow, after that, I relaxed: not much, but a little. My breathing was still fast and my eyes darted this way and that; I was positive that someone would rush out to point at us, shout *Car thieves! Arrest those car thieves!* But no one did. I watched the neighborhood pass by, everything looking strange and different now. I was riding in a stolen car, I realized. Lucy had *stolen* it—we both had. Yet with the fear there was an exhilaration too, a feeling that as long as I was with Lucy, everything was all right. Nothing would happen. As long as she was there, the darkness was safe.

Soon enough she had driven around the block and pulled up in front of Mr. Griffin's house again, exactly where the van had been parked before. We came to a very sudden stop, Lucy hitting the brakes too hard; I pitched forward in the seat, bumped my head against the dashboard.

"Sorry," she said. "I gotta practice stopping."

"Lucy, let's get out of here!" I pushed open the passenger door, dropped onto the sidewalk, ran around to the other side. Lucy was just stepping out.

"Nice drive, huh?" she said boldly, looking at me. "Now do you believe me?"

"I believe you, I believe you! Let's get out of here! My uncle is probably there by now!"

We charged back to Lucy's house and clambered through the window as quietly as we could. As Lucy replaced the screen I looked at her clock and realized that the entire adventure had taken hardly twenty minutes. My uncle wasn't even due for half an hour.

I collapsed breathlessly onto the bed, my fear returning even as I realized we'd done it: we'd gone out into the night against the rules, we'd *stolen a car,* we'd returned and not been caught. The thought was unbelievable. And we'd done it together: however reluctant I'd been, I was there, I'd done it with her. She could never deny me that, never call me a *fraidy cat* again.

After she'd closed the window, Lucy dropped down on the bed next to me. She was breathing hard too, from the excitement, from the run home. In a moment she started to giggle. It was contagious: soon I was giggling too. Then we burst into laughter, crazy laughter, we threw our arms around each other rolled around and jumped up and down and laughed, laughed as if we would never stop laughing, never in this world.

If Lucy hadn't gotten the sniffles, things might have ended completely differently.

But she did, and a couple of days after our daring auto

heist I found myself in the uncomfortable position of being at school without her. Melissa, Susan, and Miriam noticed this immediately, of course, yet on the first day they did nothing more than offer a few furtively whispered *Lezzie!* or *Where's your girlfriend?* remarks in the hallway. I kept to myself, stayed away from the bathroom, made sure I wasn't too far from a teacher during recess and lunch. I minded my own business, and they went about theirs.

But on the second day, too, Lucy didn't appear at the bus stop. I'd seen her the night before, though Ms. Sparrow suggested I not spend too long there, and I didn't. It was just a cold; Lucy's eyes were red and her nose was congested.

"I'll try to be back tomorrow," she said. Then, smiling: "Not that I'm in a big hurry."

"School's no good without you," I said, and I meant it. My life-long love of learning, my feelings of pride with each A, had largely evaporated. The day before I had actually received a C—*a C!*—on a Math quiz. I didn't care. I just wanted to be near Lucy, no matter what. I'd stopped caring about much else.

But she wasn't there that second morning, so I resigned myself to another day of dreariness. But the dreariness ended during recess, when the teacher on duty was distracted by a scuffle happening between boys on the football field. Melissa, Susan, and Miriam took this opportunity to corner me by the Social Studies classroom, where no one else could see. The three of them backed me against the wall, careful to not touch me, never actually hurting me.

"Well, look here. It's *Frances*," Melissa said.

"It's *Concentration Camp*," Susan amended.

"Where's your big ugly girlfriend?" asked Miriam.

"Shut up," I said, trying to peer around the corner to see if the teacher had returned, but she hadn't.

"Well, you've got a *mouth*," Melissa said.

"She learned it from her lezzie lover," Susan said. "She talks like that too."

"I said shut *up*," I repeated. I could hardly believe the words were coming out of me, but I'd changed in the past weeks, become bolder. Before, my reaction might have been to burst into tears; but Lucy always said I cried too much. I wasn't going to cry this time.

"Hey," Miriam said, punching me on the shoulder, "who do you think you're talking to, anyway?"

"Shut your stupid face!"

They were genuinely taken aback. They looked at each other, considering. Then they realized that they outnumbered me by a wide margin, and recovered.

"You're *rude*," Melissa said, slapping my lightly on the cheek. "Does your mom know you talk like that?"

I batted her palm away, enraged.

"Yeah," Susan said, shoving me in the chest, "does she? *I* heard you don't even *have* a mom."

"*Shut up!*"

They all giggled, completely in control again.

"She's probably dead," Miriam speculated. "Probably she killed herself when she realized she had such a dork for a kid."

"Is that it, Frances?" Susan shoved me again. "Did your mom kill herself because you're such a dork?"

What happened next happened very quickly. I heard footsteps running toward us and I knew, somehow I *knew*, whose they were. The three girls all turned simultaneously. Lucy came charging up, the look on her face so furious that even I was scared, and yet I knew she was there to protect me.

"You're *absent*," Susan said, her voice suddenly pleading in a *No fair!* kind of tone.

"My mom let me sleep late," Lucy said quietly. I could hear that her nose was still stuffed up. "I'm here now."

If they'd backed off then, as they obviously should have, things would also have been different. But they couldn't face the prospect of being humiliated in front of someone as unimportant as me, and so, disastrously, they took the plunge.

Melissa said, "So you came to help out your little girlfriend, huh, Lucy?"

Lucy looked at her, her eyes hard, cold. "Melissa," she said, "you are a worthless piece of shit."

Melissa's eyes widened.

"Hey," Miriam protested, "you can't—"

Things blurred; I never knew who moved first, but Susan shoved me against the wall hard and someone pushed me down. There was scuffling. A foot kicked me. Then I heard a huge *crack* and everything, for one seemingly endless moment suspended in time, went completely silent.

I looked up.

Melissa was standing there, mouth agape, arms dangling in mid-air. Blood ran from her nose, a nose that suddenly looked different, bent to the side, off-center. Lucy stood close to her, also frozen, her face registering the shock of what she'd just done.

Panic. Two girls rushing off: *Lucy hit Melissa! Lucy hit Melissa! Melissa's bleeding! Lucy hit Melissa!* Melissa bursting into tears mixed with wailing screams, blood running down her chin and her hands on her face and then coming away covered with blood, blood on her shirt then, blood everywhere, and I, even I feeling desperately sorry for her, for her obvious pain, frightened at the sight of the blood leaking out of her face, and Lucy frozen there for a moment, breathing hard, her fists still curled so tightly that her knuckles had turned a ghastly white.

She looked at me then, her eyes huge.

"Lucy—" I whispered.

But she turned and ran away then, back up the hall toward the street. Melissa had stumbled away toward the playground, toward the teacher, and I was left alone, halfway between the world of school, responsibility, and the world of Lucy— whatever world that was. Of course it was no competition. I got up and ran after Lucy.

—Nine—

A S I WOKE I turned to drape my arm over Donald, as always, and found that he wasn't there, as always; but the absence felt different this time, smelled different. Something was wrong.

I opened my eyes, and remembered.

The night clerk, a pimply kid, maybe twenty, tall, gawky-thin, standing there at the counter the night before, around one in the morning. The place silent, tomblike. I'd just returned from my unsuccessful hunt for Mike McCoy's old shack—my hunt for Lucy Sparrow's ghost—and felt cut off from the world, completely alone. Somewhere my life had gone wrong, I knew, and I'd never been able to get it turned right again. The closest had been the early years with Donald and Jess, when those shadows of the past had seemed furthest from me, as far away as they'd ever been. But they all came roaring back, finally, and left me overwhelmed, almost unable to walk or even stand. There were times that I pictured myself driving off a cliff somewhere, crashing into the Pacific Ocean and sinking away to cold airless darkness. There were times I pictured climbing the stairs of a tall building—any building would do—and leaping from it, spiraling, rolling down through the air and most assuredly dead when I hit the ground.

A conversation with the pimply kid. Alone with him in the hotel lobby, not a soul anywhere near. I was half drunk. Stupid small talk, stupid flirting talk. At some point I asked him if he had a girlfriend and he said no, though it wouldn't have mattered if he'd said yes. I'd done this before. I asked him to come to my room when he was off work. I was old to him, old enough to be his mother, yet not unattractive in my way, slender, a good face, and of course my dimples, those accidents of birth that have always been my main claim to cuteness.

Heading up to the room alone, knowing he'd follow me when he closed the office. And he did. There he was in the doorway, nervous, perspiring, yet I felt no nerves at all. I brought him in, pulled off his jacket, gave him a glass of wine.

I have one condition, I told him.

What?

That you stay until morning. That you be here when I wake up in the morning.

Of course he said he would.

Stay until I wake in the morning.

Of course he didn't.

I felt desolate again, emptied-out, ruined, as I always did after these sorts of encounters. A few hours of touch, of grasping and holding, of having someone, anyone, close—was it worth it? I could almost hear the tales he would tell his young pals, the old story every young male hotel clerk probably told about the liquored-up lady who'd invited him to her room, doffed her clothes, splashed into bed with him. Only in this case the story was actually true. I would be the object of jokes, of course. But that was nothing new for me.

The sex was just something to be endured—it didn't last long, anyway; it never did with very young men—for the rest, the caressing afterward, the soft meaningless love words. And he'd been nice enough in that way. But of course he was gone now. He might come to a pathetic middle-aged woman's bed in the middle of the night, but he certainly wouldn't want to be caught there the next morning, in the harsh glare of daylight.

In my mind I could hear Lucy and me talking, these unvisited memories from thirty years ago that were crashing over me again so astonishingly:

I could get married. I think I could. Someday.

To a man? And—and you'd have sex with him?

To my surprise, my cell phone chirped.

"Hello?"

"Mom?"

I inhaled sharply, sat up in the bed.

"Jess?"

"Yeah."

"I—I'm so glad to hear from you, honey. What's…?"

"Dad said I should call you. I'm not doing it because I want to."

"Well, okay," I said, trying to control my breathing, which had suddenly become quick and shallow. I wanted to reach through the phone, to take her in my arms, hold on. "I understand, honey."

"Anyway, happy birthday. That's what I called to say."

"Happy…? But it's not my birthday."

"Well, Dad says it is."

"Well, Dad is…" And then I realized: It *was* my birthday. "Oh my God," I said, "I completely forgot. Can you believe that? I just got up, and…"

"Just got *up*? It's almost lunchtime."

"I—" And I realized that she was right about that, too. "Well, I—I haven't been feeling well. I'm traveling, you know, and I'm kind of tired. I'm in California."

"Why?" Her voice was bored, but it was a voice, it was *her* voice.

"I had a book festival in Santa Barbara," I said. "It's a beautiful place, Jess. Right on the ocean. I'd like to take you there sometime."

"Mm."

"Why—Jess, why are you calling now? Aren't you in school?"

"It's Sunday, Mom. Jesus, you're really spaced out, you know?"

I laughed, a little. "You're right, honey. I forgot. I'm—I'm not in Santa Barbara right now, actually. I drove north a ways, to a little town called Quiet. Isn't that a funny name? Quiet?"

"Why?"

"I used to live here when I was young. When I was your age, actually." I could picture her on the other end of the phone lying on her father and stepmother's couch, baseball cap on her head, twirling her hair in her fingers, blowing bubblegum bubbles. "I've been…just visiting places I used to know."

"Sounds boring."

"Oh, well…It would be, honey, probably, to you. But it's interesting to me."

"Well, okay. Whatever. Happy birthday. I'm going to hang up now."

"Jess?" I clutched the phone tightly, tightly. "Jess, honey, I—could we talk for a couple of minutes? Please?"

"I'm kind of busy, Mom."

"I—I know, but…Just for a minute or two. I just…"

"What?" I heard a light popping noise on the line that might have been her gum bubble bursting next to the receiver.

"I—" But suddenly I knew that I couldn't just tell her I was sorry again. I couldn't just tell her how much I loved her or how I wanted us to be close again. She'd heard all that. It meant nothing to her. She was a kid who'd been hurt, betrayed over and over, and it amazed me to realize that I was the one who had done it, just as it had been done to me all those years before.

"Honey, I—" I tried to start again. I felt that what I would say was terribly important and yet I was weak, confused. I was naked in a hotel room bed, disheveled, bleary-headed, yet I was supposed to be a parent now, somehow, I was supposed to say something that would have meaning to the person I'd hurt the most, the very person I'd never meant to hurt at all.

"Mom, just forget it, whatever it is."

"No, I—I want to tell you. I—"

"Goddamn it, Mom, you always do this."

"No, honey…"

"Happy birthday, that's all I have to say. Goodbye."

"No—"

But she was gone.

I started to call her back, but I knew it was no use. After a moment I put the phone down again, sat up. I looked at the bottle of wine that was still sitting on the table. It was half full. I was about to reach to it when my phone chirped again. I grabbed it.

"Jess?"

"It's Donald, Frances."

"Oh." I hoped my disappointment wasn't too obvious in my voice.

"I just wanted you to know—I overheard the call, Jess has turned on the TV now, she can't hear me—I just wanted you to know that she lied about something."

"What's that?"

"I didn't tell her to call you. I'll admit that I reminded her it was your birthday—happy birthday, by the way—but I didn't tell her to call you. I didn't say a thing about it."

I breathed shakily. "Donald—is that the truth?"

"Yes. I—look, we're getting ready to go out, but I wanted you to know that. Okay?"

"Yes," I said. I clenched my eyes shut, felt myself trembling.

"Yes, Donald, okay. Thank you for telling me."

Blackstone Road leads northeast out of Quiet past isolated homes with long driveways and big front yards, SUVs and speedboats before them. But after a few miles the houses vanish; the road narrows and pine trees and wild grasses seem to close in. It's a lovely semi-rural drive, if rather a lonely one.

Sarah Shaw's address had been easy to find on the Internet; what hadn't been so easy was figuring out what I would say to her, or how. I'd considered phoning her, even writing her a letter, but in the end I decided to just drive to her home and knock on the door.

Different plans had bounced through my mind. I might pretend to be someone else—I could certainly say I was a writer, which was true enough. I could claim I was writing a book on serial killers and would like to speak to her about her brother. Were they close? Did she hear from him? How had she reacted when she'd learned of the crimes?

And where was he now?

But of course it wasn't Sarah Shaw to whom I really wanted to speak. Yet I suspected she would be highly protective of her brother, shielding him from inquiries like mine—which must, after all, come along now and then; Mike McCoy was not among the notorious elite of serial killers, but surely a few researchers or would-be true crime bestseller writers had been out here over the years, trying to find him. Probably it would prove impossible. And what, after all, did I want with him?

Even now I wasn't sure. But something, something had gone wrong in my life all those years before, and in retracing my steps I felt that I might somehow put it right, readjust myself so that I might live the remainder of my days in some kind of peace. My parents were long dead; there was no peace available there. But when I was twelve—that was when everything collapsed, when I was hurled wailing into a black tunnel from which I'd never, I realized now, quite escaped. I didn't know what I sought. But I was compelled to seek it.

I considered the call from Jess. A lifeline, I thought. It hadn't gone that well, but she'd called. She'd wished me a happy birthday, called me *Mom* when, for a very long time, she'd called me nothing at all. It was some kind of start. But I knew that I had no more chances left with her after this one. Her father was wonderful to her and her stepmother had proven herself a gifted parent. Jess had no use for me, not really; the only thread that kept us together was the fact that I was her mother. But that thread could snap, I knew. It *would* snap if I screwed up again. And what's more, if I did, it should: Jess deserved better than me.

I thought of the pimply-faced boy the night before, no doubt believing he was getting something special with me; quite possibly I took his virginity. How sad, I thought, to have only me as a memory of that. How little he understood what he'd had in that bed, how quickly he would have run away instead of jabbing himself into me with his quick, anxious thrusts. I thought of the poor saps who had stood in the book-signing lines to meet me: not the children (who were too young to really understand where books came from anyway), but their parents, who would smile and compliment me and tell me what a difference Flat-Head Fred and Mary the Motor Scooter had made for their kids. I would smile right back, show my dimples, sign the books, think: *If you only knew.*

At last I began to see the occasional mailbox at the edge of the road. The houses were still far back, but now there were no SUVs or speedboats: a few miles made an obvious difference in social class. These were older, smaller, run-down homes with dirt driveways holding old dented cars and pickups.

At last I saw the box: *Shaw.*

I pulled in. The yard and house reminded me strangely of the Sparrows' place, all those years ago: grime, disorder, garbage in the yard (though it was mostly weeds, hardly a yard at all). I felt my heart beating as I stopped the car and stepped out. I inhaled. I had my story: researcher, true crime, serial killers, could we talk? I could even tell her, quite honestly, that I had a contract with a major publisher in New York. I wouldn't mention that it was for the next two Fred and Mary titles.

Their house had an old but serviceable front porch and a crumpled screen door hanging on rusty hinges. Rather than pausing, rather than thinking about anything, I just knocked.

I had no idea who would answer the door. Did she even live here anymore? Yes, she must—the name *Shaw* was on the mailbox, after all. There was only one Sarah Shaw anywhere in the area. And yet what if the librarian had been wrong? What if Sarah Shaw wasn't Mike McCoy's sister at all? What if—

The door opened a crack and I saw an eye, very dark, very suspicious, peering out at me.

"Yes?"

"I—um, Mrs. Shaw?"

"Yes?"

"My—my name is Frances Pastan," I said, trying to keep my voice steady. "I'm a writer and I'm doing…doing research on, well, serial—serial killers…"

"Christ," I heard the voice say.

"And I'm wondering—that is, I'm hoping that—"

"I haven't talked to the son of a bitch in twenty years."

"I—excuse me, Mrs. Shaw, you mean—?"

"My brother. That's who you want, isn't it? I haven't talked to him in twenty years. Son of a bitch was living around Vegas somewhere, last I heard. I can't tell you anything else.

Goodbye."

And the door shut. I heard the dead bolt being turned.

I stood there dumbly, almost without thought. I was tempted to knock again, to apologize, to explain, but realized that there was no point. She'd said all she would say.

But she'd given me a place.

—Ten—

IT WAS A major event at Soames Elementary School that year, easily eclipsing the soccer team's championship in its division and the afternoon assembly at which a minor but recognizable TV actor appeared to tell us to "stay off the dope." Lucy was suspended, of course; there was talk of her being expelled or even arrested. I was made to report to the principal's office with my uncle—I pleaded with him to come rather than my aunt—and Mr. Blatt discussed the possibility of suspending me, too: an astonishing, surreal idea for a girl who, until recently, had panicked if she received an A-minus on a quiz. But then the principal admitted that, having talked to Susan and Miriam and their parents—Melissa was in the hospital—it was clear to him that those girls had started the whole thing. My only crime had been in running away from school after it happened, and Mr. Blatt was willing to forgive that—"*this* time," he said warningly.

I took some pleasure in the fact that Susan and Miriam were being suspended as well, though only for a day—quite unlike the solid week's sentence Lucy had received. (Melissa's fate would be decided when she was well enough to return.) But it made school the next day positively bizarre. Four girls had suddenly vanished, depleting our already small classes. The other kids looked at me with something like awe: I was the only one to have actually been in the middle of the firestorm, to have survived it and to have returned unscathed. The belief seemed to be that Lucy and I had taken on the three girls in something like a tag-team wrestling match; they had no idea

131

I'd simply been knocked down and kicked.

I, meanwhile, had no idea that this would prove to be my last of all days at Soames Elementary.

My complete innocence in the situation didn't affect my aunt, of course, who grounded me with the instruction to "never, *never* talk to that horrible Sparrow girl again." I knew better than to argue with her when she was in high dudgeon. She railed on for a long time, marching back and forth in front of me as I sat on the bed in my room. Waving her Marlboro around wildly she said terrible things about Lucy, terrible things about Ms. Sparrow, terrible things about me, but none of it mattered. I hardly heard it. There seemed to be a dark chasm opening where my future had once stood. Would Lucy be allowed back to school? What if she were expelled? Where would she go? Could she really be *arrested*?

"I mean it, Frances. Don't have anything to do with that horrible girl. You've changed since you became friends with her. Well, now I hope you see just who it is you've been friends with. She *broke* that pretty little Deaver girl's *nose.* Do you understand, Frances? She broke her nose! That's a *major thing*! That's…that's *assault and battery*!" She stopped pacing, stood still for a moment. "That little girl will never look the same, Frances. That's what your friend did. A broken nose never looks the same afterward, no matter how well they set it. That girl will be dealing with that *forever*."

"Good," I whispered, though much too softly for my aunt to hear.

"Well, I hope you're happy about this, that's all I can say," she said at last, and stalked out of the room, slamming the door, leaving the odor of cigarette smoke behind.

I was too overwhelmed, too emotional for tears. I just sat on my bed and trembled. For a while my life had seemed to make sense: my parents had gotten rid of me, my aunt and uncle were only figureheads, but with Lucy I had a life, a real life that was more important than school or anything else. Now it was in jeopardy. All I wanted to do at that moment was see her, talk to her, tell her that things would be all right (but I didn't know that they would be all right, I didn't know that at all). Awful things seemed to be happening now, things beyond her control or mine. Erratic, inscrutable grown-ups would make decisions which would affect us both forever. Nothing but darkness and terror seemed to lie ahead.

I dozed for a time; I didn't sleep. Evil visions leapt at me: my father slamming the door in my face after I had a glimpse of my mother, rubber tubing wrapped around her arm, syringe sticking out of it; my aunt, her voice hard and unforgiving, the glowing cigarette waving madly in the air; Melissa and Susan and Miriam, their pretty faces contorted and ugly now, taunting me, pushing me down. But I couldn't see Lucy at all, couldn't conjure her face or voice in my mind. She was lost to me in this churning ocean of darkness and terror.

I was brought out of my uneasy trance-like state by, of all things, a soft knocking on my window.

I was startled, but only for an instant. I realized immediately who it must be. I ran to the window, pulled away the curtains. She was there, her face glowing whitely, ghostlike against the dark. I pulled open the window and touched the screen with my hand; she touched it too. Our palms pushed together, only the mesh between us.

"Lucy!" I whispered.

In my joy at seeing her it took me a moment to realize that she was crying. I'd never seen her cry; it was shocking, another new impossible thing to be thrown at me in the past couple of days. How could Lucy be crying? I was the one who cried, too much.

"Can you come outside?" she whispered, her voice

trembling.

"Lucy, I—what time is it?" I glanced back to my desk clock: almost exactly one o'clock in the morning.

I looked at her again. Her eyes were red, her mouth twisted. Tears had run down her cheeks, making them glisten. Her hair was wild, askew.

Of course I went. I'd never undone the screen on my own window, but it turned out to be exactly the same as Lucy's and came away easily. I was still dressed, never having really gone to bed. I climbed through the window, dropped into the backyard, turned and slid the window mostly shut again.

Lucy walked off into the backyard in the direction of the pepper tree, the darkness seeming to swallow her. She wore her black Bachman-Turner Overdrive T-shirt and blue jeans. It was a cool night, early spring. I followed her, a strange thrill thrumming in my bones. I'd never been outside this late. I'd never visited the pepper tree in the dark. But it was no time for fun: she leaned against one of the main branches, slumped there, crying quietly and looking completely defeated.

"Lucy, what is it?" I whispered. "What's wrong? Are they—are they going to *arrest* you?"

She looked at me then, snorted with miserable laughter. "No, they're not gonna arrest me, Fran." She sniffed, cleared her throat, trying to bring her tears under control.

"You should have been at school today," I said. "It was so weird. You, Melissa, Susan, Miriam—everybody was gone. And everybody else was looking at *me*."

"Oh, yeah?" she said, uninterested.

"Yeah," I said, aware that her mind was on something else but unable to figure out what else to say to her. "Melissa's in the hospital. Well, I think they let her out today. Susan and Miriam were suspended for a day. They'll be back tomorrow, I guess."

"Did you get in trouble?" she asked, her voice distant.

"I had to go to Mr. Blatt's office with my uncle. He didn't suspend me, though."

"That's good."

"Lucy—" I reached out, then stopped, my hand dangling in mid-air. "Lucy, what is it?"

She looked at me, her silver-gray eyes glistening in the dark. "Can you keep a secret?"

"Sure I can. You don't have to ask me that, Lucy."

She looked away, picked at the bark of the pepper tree's trunk. "My mom and me are moving."

I felt a terrible free-fall sensation in the pit of my stomach.

"*Moving?*" I gasped.

"Yeah."

We stood there. A breeze pushed a few pepper leaves in my face, tickling my cheek.

"Lucy, why? Is it this…this thing with Melissa? I'm sure Mr. Blatt will let you come back, Lucy. Boys get in fights all the time and they—"

"It's not that," she said. "It's not that at all. That doesn't matter now. It's not even important."

"Well, then what?"

"My fucking *dad,*" she said, practically spitting the word. As she said it she dropped suddenly to the ground, sat lotus-legged on the floor of our little personal forest. I fell to my knees beside her.

"What about your dad, Lucy?"

She didn't look at me. "My mom thinks he's found us."

"Found you? What do you mean? What are you talking about?"

"I mean *found us.* So we have to move again."

"Lucy, I don't get it. Why do you have to leave because

your dad found you?"

She scowled at me and I was sure she was about to call me stupid, but instead she reached to her jaw and ran her finger down the long line there that I'd once taken for a birthmark.

"'Cuz of this," she said. "'Cuz my dad put it there. And lots of others, too."

"He…?"

She sighed shakily, but in talking seemed to regain her composure. "That's what my dad does when he gets drunk. He gets crazy. He knocked my mom out once. I still remember the sound of the punch and coming into the room and seeing her there on the floor, not moving, like a pile of old garbage. And my dad coming at me with a kitchen knife in his hand. He grabbed me, pulled my head back by the hair, and—well, I don't remember the rest. That was just the last time. He'd done it before." She picked at pepper leaves on the ground. "Knives. Lit cigarettes. He was always careful to do it where it wouldn't show, until the last time."

We sat there silently. I could hear crickets chirping. I didn't know what to say. I had absolutely no idea what on earth I could possibly say.

She took the little pepper leaves into her fingers and slowly tore them apart, studying each closely, holding them to her nose and breathing in their spicy odor. "When I was being punished," she said, her voice strangely calm now, dispassionate, "one thing he used to do was make me pull my pants down and then stick things into me. The toilet paper roller or the handle of a screwdriver or something like that. In my butt. In my privates. He'd say, 'This is what happens to bad girls, Lucy.' He'd do it when Mom wasn't home and then tell me he'd stick a gun in there the next time if I said anything. He has a gun, too. A couple of 'em."

After a moment she added expressionlessly, "Anyway,

we're moving."

I swallowed. "Why isn't he is jail, Lucy?"

"Oh, he's been there. They let him out. One month, two months, six months. They always let him out. And he comes looking for us…I'm not from around here, you know. I'm not from anywhere around here. I grew up in Wyoming. Near Casper." She was silent for a time. Then: "Do you believe in God?"

"Um…" I hesitated. "I don't know. Sometimes I do."

"Know what I think?" she asked, looking at the sky. "I think that there are people that God hates."

"Why would He hate people, Lucy?"

"Well, why does He love people—some people? Who knows? Who knows why God does anything? Why does He let wars happen? Why does He let little babies starve? I mean, God is everything, right? He's everything and everywhere."

"I—I don't know. He's supposed to be, I guess."

"If He's everything, then He's not just love, He's hate, too. And I think that there are just some people that God hates. That's the only way to understand the things that happen in the world. When I hear about a bad thing happening to somebody I just can't help but think: God must've hated that person."

We were quiet for a moment.

"My parents use drugs," I blurted out.

Lucy looked at me.

"That's why they got rid of me," I said. "They use…heroin and things like that. And they sell it. They think I don't know about it, but I do. We live in this nice house with a maid and everything but they're…dope pushers," I said, remembering the phrase from the school assembly. "I always thought dope pushers were, like, weird dirty people on street corners. But my dad owns a store, a nice one—three of them. Like a chain.

They sell radios and stereos and, like, electronic stuff there." I had never told anyone about my parents. No one. But Lucy's revelations seemed to demand my own. "My mom, she—she actually worked as a model for magazines. But that was a long time ago. Now she's a—" I could hardly believe I was saying it, but out it came—"My mom's a drug addict. They're just… messed up. Both of them."

We sat silently together.

"I don't wanna move again," Lucy announced finally. "I hate moving. I never have any friends. I don't know anybody. My mom…I love my mom, but she's just—I dunno. She's talking about us going to fuckin' *Mexico*." She was silent for a moment. "Her life would be better if I wasn't around. He always hit me more than he did her. I think…I think if I wasn't there he might not come after her at all. Crap, maybe I should just kill myself. I'm not worth anything to anybody."

"You are," I said, "to me."

She smiled then, weakly. "Aw, Franny-Fran," she said, tossing the leaves away.

"I think we should—" But I didn't finish the thought.

"Should what?"

I looked away. "Nothing," I said.

She sat forward, studying me closely. "C'mon, what?"

"Never mind."

"You're thinking about Mr. Griffin's van, aren't you?"

"No," I lied. Then: "Yes."

"So am I."

"Where would we go, Lucy?"

"I dunno. Who cares? Away from this place. Malibu, maybe. Santa Barbara. Those beaches. Hollywood. I told you, I wanna meet John Travolta."

"Do you think you could?"

"Why not? I'd just walk up to him on Sunset Boulevard or

whatever and say, 'Hi, Johnny-Boy, I'm Lucy.'"

I smiled. "You wouldn't call him Johnny-Boy."

"The heck I wouldn't. Of course with my luck we'd probably never see him at all. We'd probably see goddamn *Donny Osmond* instead."

"Donny Osmond is cute," I insisted.

"Donny Osmond looks just like his sister Marie," she said contemptuously. "They must be twins. Those awful buck teeth."

"They're not buck teeth. They're just big."

"Buck."

"Big."

"Buck!"

She shoved me on my shoulder and we giggled.

"Do you think we could?" I asked finally.

"What?"

"Make it to Hollywood."

"Maybe. Malibu, at least."

"What would we do when we got there?"

"I dunno. Somethin'. Maybe we can get on a TV show. *You* could. With your dimples."

There was suddenly what felt like a current of electricity between us. We were about to jump off a cliff together. This was the last moment to pull back.

"Do you want to?" Lucy asked quietly.

"I don't know. Do you?"

"If you come with me, yeah."

"Really?"

"Well, it wouldn't be any fun alone, would it?"

"No, I guess not."

We looked at each other.

"C'mon," Lucy said, jumping up. "C'mon, right now, before we chicken out!"

The first moment of terror came when I realized that we mustn't go without anything at all: we would need food, money. I found myself crawling back into my room again and then rushing barefoot into the kitchen, grabbing a box of crackers, some fruit, and several cans of soda pop, pushing them into my rucksack along with a few toiletry items: hairbrush, soap, toothbrush, toothpaste. Finally I returned to my room, slipped on my shoes, and took what little money I'd saved—it was about thirty dollars—from where I kept it in my desk and stuffed the bills into my pockets. At last I climbed outside again to where Lucy was waiting. I slid the window completely shut, locking myself out of my own house. But I knew I was never coming back.

"C'mon!" Lucy whispered breathlessly.

We ran giggling up the street. What we would have done had Mr. Griffin's van not been in its usual spot, or if the keys had been missing, I don't know; we would have been crushed beyond words, certainly. But it didn't happen.

"Shh. He's home," Lucy said, pointing at the car in Mr. Griffin's driveway. "We'll have to be really quiet."

"What if he hears the van start?"

"If he hears it, he hears it. Look, he's asleep. His lights are off. He won't hear anything."

We stood next to the van and Lucy peered in. "The keys are in it!" she whispered triumphantly.

"Okay," I said.

"Get in the other side," she instructed. "Open the door as quietly as you can and don't close it."

"Don't close it?"

"We'll close the doors just as soon as we get a little ways from the house. He might hear the doors slamming."

I ran around the side and jumped in, held the door handle in my hand.

"Here goes nothing," she said, her eyes wild with excitement. She turned the key. The van's engine burst into life, as loud, I imagined, as a supersonic jet. She put the vehicle in gear and eased slowly off the clutch until we were sliding slowly forward on the street. After we'd traveled perhaps fifty yards she said, "Okay, close 'em!" and we shut the doors. I locked mine. Neither of us bothered to put on seatbelts.

We rolled through the neighborhood streets, Lucy focused completely on the road before her. She turned on the lights. My heart was pounding. My mouth was dry. I was perspiring, even though I felt cold. My eyes darted about, searching for the police car I was sure would come roaring up to us with a policeman sticking his head out the window and pointing his gun toward us, shouting, *Pull over! Pull over!*

But the drive through the neighborhood was as uneventful as a drive with an unlicensed twelve-year-old driver can be. There were no cars in front or behind us; none approached us from the opposite direction. The van's flatulent engine was loud but the world outside seemed silent, still, lifeless, like a dead city on the moon. I inhaled as Lucy made the final turn out of the housing tract and we moved onto Bridgewater Avenue, the bridge itself looming before us. I wondered what it would be like if she were to lose control of the vehicle, smash into the guardrail and send us careening over the edge into the riverbed a hundred feet below. Would we have time to scream? Would the impact kill us instantly, or would we survive for a few minutes, blood leaking everywhere from our shattered bodies? I thought of the girls who had been found in the riverbed recently, their corpses, their mutilated faces, flies on their lips, river rats chewing on their cheeks. Death seemed very close.

And yet Lucy negotiated the bridge perfectly. We were moving very slowly—she hadn't shifted out of first gear.

142 - Christopher Conlon

But once we were over the bridge she did. The gears made a bad grinding sound for a moment and we slowed nearly to a stop, but then she found second and we lurched forward. We were moving a bit faster now as we pulled through the town. Nothing was open. There were no people anywhere. This seemed a completely different world than the one that Lucy and I rode through in the daytime. The darkness covered everything, sucked the life from it, obliterated it. Lucy and I were the only two people in the world, it seemed. I was terrified. I was happy.

Eventually we neared the freeway. Lucy glanced at me; I smiled and said nothing. I was with her all the way now; there was no turning back. If we ran off the road, if we died fiery deaths, we would do it together. We passed the familiar rest stop and I looked at the oak tree, the grass, the building. I wouldn't miss any of it, I thought. All I could ever miss in my broken-up life was here, in this van, sitting beside me, taking me away to a place where we would stay together forever. I was exactly where I should be, where I had to be.

"We want to go south, right?" Lucy asked, her expression pensive.

"Yeah," I said. "South."

She followed the sign for *U.S. 101 South*. It led us onto a big loose curve that Lucy took very slowly. When it ended it merged straight into the freeway and we, giddy with excitement, were suddenly on it. We were on the *freeway!*

The problem was that we weren't moving very fast. Lucy kept the vehicle in second gear as one car and then another came whizzing up behind us only to swerve into the left lane and pass us by. One honked.

"Lucy, we…we'd better go faster!"

"Yeah, um…" She hesitated. "Actually I've never gotten past second gear. I don't really know how."

I looked at her. "Don't you think," I said, "you should have thought of that before?"

"Well, I didn't!" She glanced at me uneasily. I found myself giggling, through sheer nervous energy.

But then a huge truck, an eighteen-wheeler, came roaring up behind us. In the passenger's side rear-view mirror I could see it sweeping up to us at frightening speed. I thought it was going to crash into our van, but at the last moment, horn blaring, it changed lanes and blew past us.

"Lucy, come on, we really have to go faster! Somebody will hit us!"

"I know, I know. My mom showed me once…It's like an 'H.' " She outlined the motion with her hand. "First is here, second is here…then you, like, push it up, then to the right, and then up again. Yeah. That's it. I'm sure of it. Okay." She pushed in the clutch and took the gear shift in her hand. She tugged at it, but nothing happened except the awful grinding noise. The van slowed down even more. "Shit! *Shit!*" she cried, pushing and pulling at the thing. Finally she slipped the vehicle back into second.

"I can't find it," she admitted.

"Let me try," I said.

"You? What do you know about it?"

"Well, I can't do any worse than you! It's like the top part of the 'H,' right?"

"Yeah. Up, over to the right, and then up again. Supposedly."

I leaned over and took the gearshift in both my hands. "How will I know if I've done it right?"

"The grinding noise will stop!"

"Oh. Right."

"Ready?"

"Yeah."

"You sure?"

"Yeah!"

She pushed in the clutch and I, ever the dutiful student, pushed the gear shift up, to the right, and then up again. It slid in perfectly, and the van smoothly began to speed up.

"Franny, you did it!" Lucy cried. "You *did* it!"

I laughed again, almost hysterically. Lucy was behind the wheel but I was helping. I was helping to *drive*. I was helping to drive our *stolen car*.

"How many gears are there?" I asked, my nerves jumping, wild. "Do you want to try another?"

"No," she said. "Not yet. We're okay now. People are still passing us but it's not bad now. Look—we're going forty."

I gazed at the speedometer and then through the windshield. The roadway seemed to be sucked under the van as we rode.

"I can't believe we're actually doing this!" I said finally.

She laughed. "Neither can I!"

Another car passed us on the left. Aghast, I realized that it was a police car.

"Oh my God! Lucy!"

"I don't think he sees us," she said, breathing quickly. She was as nervous as I was. "I think we're okay. Everybody knows these VW vans are slow, anyway." And indeed, the car passed us by.

We drove for nearly an hour like that. We didn't shift again. The road was straight, for the most part; what curves there were had the grace to be gentle, easy for Lucy to negotiate. Eventually we came over a rise in the road and saw the Pacific Ocean off to our right: an immense black expanse that stretched nearly to eternity.

"The *ocean*!" we cried simultaneously, and laughed.

Quiet was only twenty miles or so inland, but my aunt

and uncle had certainly never bothered to take me to the sea. The sight was astonishing, unbelievable. "There's nothing like this in Fresno!" I said. "It's so *big*!"

We rode in satisfied silence for a time.

"Is Malibu far?" I asked.

"I dunno," Lucy said. "Maybe a sign'll tell us soon." Then, suddenly: "Oh, *crap*!"

"What? What's wrong?"

She looked at me sickly. "I just noticed. We're almost out of gas."

She pointed to the gauge. I leaned over and saw that the needle was directly over the *E*.

I thought. "Maybe there'll be a gas station."

"I don't know how to put *gas* in this thing. Do you?"

"No," I admitted. "Maybe we could get full service. I've got money."

"Fran, what's the gas station guy gonna think when *we* pull up?"

"Well…you look older than you are, Lucy."

"I don't look old enough to be driving *this* thing."

We kept on, both of us frozen in indecision.

"Well, shit," she said at last, "We have to do *something*. I don't wanna run out of gas right here on the freeway!"

"Lucy, look," I said, pointing. "There's an exit. It looks like it goes down to the beach."

She glanced at me. "You think we should take it?"

I swallowed. "It's better than running out of gas out here."

"Okay," she said. "Here goes nothing."

She swerved onto the exit ramp. The road drifted to the right toward the ocean and Lucy kept the van moving smoothly in the lane for a time. But suddenly we went into a tight turn too fast and the van began swerving between lanes.

"Lucy, slow down!"

"I'm trying!"

But she couldn't get it under control. Her eyes were wild and sweat glistened on her face; she seemed to freeze. We careened toward the beach, sideswiping a tree. Its branches clattered against my window and made me instinctively duck away. She overcorrected then, yanking the wheel suddenly; we crossed the center line, banged against the guardrail on the other side of the road. Then we lurched into the middle of the street.

"Lucy, look! A parking lot! Try to pull into it!"

She did. Mercifully it was empty; we slid uncontrollably across its many spaces, straight across the lot, heading toward a little darkened booth at the far end whose sign advertised *Hot Dogs / Cold Drinks / Bait.*

"Lucy, hit the brake, the brake!"

She must have; the tires began to squeal. We slid sideways across the end of the lot. The back end of the van clipped the corner of the snack booth hard, sending the vehicle spinning. I was thrown to the floor, my head slamming against the dashboard as I dropped. We bumped and crashed over rough terrain and then, *bang!* we suddenly stopped.

I looked up; my eyes had been clenched shut in terror. I was practically upside-down, my head on the floor, my legs splayed upward. I felt pains in my neck and back. My forehead throbbed.

Lucy had held onto the steering wheel; she still did, clutching it with both hands in a virtual death-grip. She sat there, eyes wider than I'd ever seen them, staring straight ahead, frozen. Her breathing was hard and fast.

"Oh my God," she whispered finally. It was very quiet; I realized suddenly that the motor wasn't running anymore.

"Oh my God, oh my God," she whispered again, then

looked down at me. "Oh my God, Franny-Fran, are you okay? Are you all right?"

"I'm—okay," I said, struggling to get back up into the seat.

"You're not. Your head's bleeding. Oh my God, Franny, oh my God, I'm sorry, I'm so sorry..."

"It's okay," I said, touching the spot with my fingers. It only seemed to be a little cut. "Are you okay, Lucy?"

"I—" It seemed to be the first time she'd thought about it. "I'm—I'm fine. I guess. But Fran—you—" Her eyes were still big, horrified.

"I think I'm okay, Lucy. Let's get out."

I opened the door and jumped down to the ground, which was sand. I looked around. We had managed somehow to crash into a little grove of palm trees that sat at the edge of the beach, where the road ended. It was one of those trees that had finally stopped us. I stretched, rubbed the back of my neck. I took a Kleenex I had in my pocket and dabbed the blood on my head. There wasn't much. It was a scratch.

Lucy came around to me. "Are you hurt?" she asked.

"No…Just a little sore. I'm okay, Lucy."

She looked around the darkness. "I—I could've *killed* you."

"I'm okay. It's all right."

"It's not all right." She wrapped her arms around herself. She was trembling. "*It's not all right.*"

"Lucy—"

She looked at me, eyes brimming over with tears. Then, suddenly, she ran off toward the sea.

"Lucy, wait!"

I followed her. It was a surreal feeling, the ocean monstrously huge and black before us, the sound of the waves pounding the shore, the way the beach sand seemed to want to suck me down into it. She reached the water's edge and stood there facing infinity.

She was doubled-over and weeping, as if someone had punched her in the stomach. But these weren't the quiet tears of earlier in the night; this was a deep, mournful cry, an agonized wail that seemed to contain within it all the misery of the world.

I stood behind her in the night.

"Don't cry, Lucy. Please don't cry. I—I'm supposed to be the one who cries…."

But she didn't stop. Her hair dangled over her head, obscuring her face. It shook as her body did. Standing close I could see the tears dropping from her cheeks onto the wet sand, disappearing into it.

"I'm—" she tried to say, her voice choked, "I'm—*so sorry,* Fran."

"I'm okay, Lucy," I said again. "We're both okay. It wasn't your fault."

"Yes it was!" She dropped down to the sand then, sat with her face in her hands. "It was all my fault! You never would have been here if it hadn't been for me! I'm a…I'm an *idiot!*"

I sat beside her. Our shoulders touched lightly.

I was in a strange mood, perhaps some very mild form of shock. I wasn't upset at all, about anything. I was worried that Lucy was crying, but the danger I'd been in, our hopeless future, none of it seemed important just then. The beach was completely deserted. Lucy and I were alone together and we were all right. That was all that mattered.

"Lucy," I said after a while, "look at the ocean. It's beautiful."

She stared at me, her tears slowing at last.

"How can you talk about the ocean," she said shakily, "right now?"

"What else is there to talk about, Lucy? We wanted to see the ocean, didn't we? Here we are."

She chuckled slightly then, shook her head. "Franny, you're crazy."

I smiled, shrugged. The ocean truly was beautiful. It was the most beautiful thing I'd ever seen. I felt very peaceful sitting there, looking at it with Lucy beside me.

After a while she calmed down and stared out at the ocean with me.

"They'll come get us, you know," she said.

"I know."

"I mean they really will."

"I know."

Silence between us. The ocean, surging.

"Maybe we could hide in the sand dunes," she said.

"Maybe."

"Aw, crap," she said finally. "Who am I kidding? They'd just catch us, sooner or later. This whole thing was stupid. It's all my fault."

"It wasn't stupid, Lucy."

"Well, we're in trouble now, that's for sure."

We were silent for a long time.

Finally she said, "I've got an idea." She reached into her pocket, where she kept her little billfold. She brought it out, reached into it and took the razor blade from inside. "Remember this?" she asked.

"Sure I do. Blood sisters." I smiled and held up the finger she'd pricked.

"Yeah, well…" She held out her arm, palm up. The pose reminded me of my mother with her rubber tubing and syringe. "See," she said, "this is the way you do it. Right across like this. Both arms." She drew the blade lightly across the blue veins on the inside of her wrist. She looked at me, her eyes glistening brightly. "I'll do it if you will."

I reached out my hand, took the razor blade from her. I pressed it lightly to my own wrist. I wondered what it would feel like.

Then I jumped up and threw the blade as far as I could into the sea.

Lucy came up behind me. "What'd you do *that* for?"

I just looked at her.

"Aw, crap," she said finally. "You're right. It was stupid."

We watched the ocean rolling toward us. The waves made a sizzling sound as they flattened out and slid toward our feet. There was a sudden shriek overhead—a bird? a bat?—and I looked up, startled, my fear of the dark slicing abruptly into me. But when I looked toward Lucy, she seemed not to have noticed. That calmed me again.

"Let's go swimming," she said at last.

"Now?" I asked.

"Why not?"

I smiled quizzically. "It's kind of cold. And I didn't bring a swimsuit."

"Aw, who cares? There's nobody here. We'll skinny-dip."

"You mean swim *naked*?"

"My mom and I used to do it at this lake we went to. It's fun. C'mon!"

She kicked off her shoes then and pulled off her socks. Facing away from me, she lifted off her shirt. She wasn't wearing her bra. I saw her scars immediately: jagged stripes on her shoulder blades, little raised brown spots. She pulled off her pants then. There were scars on her bottom as well.

"Well, c'mon!" she said, running a few feet toward the water, squatting in it, scooping some back at me, trying to get me wet. I squealed and backed away.

"Fraidy cat!" she called.

I pulled off my own clothes, hardly self-conscious at all. I knew that Lucy was the only person on earth I would do this for, that I *could* do this for. When I finished I scrambled into the icy surf and we splashed water at each other, shrieking and giggling. Her body was mature: she had hard little breasts, curving hips, a light-colored triangle of hair between her legs. I felt suddenly ashamed of my scrawny little girl's body—flat, angular, practically featureless.

But Lucy, looking at me, said: "You're pretty, Fran."

Then she plunged laughingly into the surf, her powerful arms pulling her past the curling waves and into the sea. I tried to keep up, but she was a much better swimmer. Dog-paddling as best I could out past the waves, I watched her arms lift and plunge, lift and plunge. They looked like an angel's wings, I thought. Soon, though, the wings seemed to shrink, to disappear, and I was alone in the darkness.

"Lucy, no," I whispered. "Lucy, please don't leave me."

I treaded water for a time, slowly growing frightened. I accidentally swallowed some cold salt water and began to cough. I started to wonder what monstrous sea-beasts were lurking just past my naked feet, ready to latch onto me with their teeth or tentacles. The sea looked huge then, the lightless sky vast—there was no moon, few stars. The sand dunes on the shore seemed to loom threateningly toward me. It was dark, so dark that it was impossible to imagine a time it would ever be light.

And then a sea-monster grabbed me. I gasped as it slipped over my ankle, rope-like and slimy. I kicked frantically at it, but only managed to bind it tighter to me. My legs were tangled in it. I flailed wildly, trying to scream, gulping saltwater.

"Lucy! Lucy!"

And somehow she was there, her glistening arm appearing around my neck from behind, her voice in my ear: "Fran, stop kicking! It's only kelp! It's *kelp,* Fran! It's seaweed! *Stop kicking*!"

But I was still struggling and swallowing water as she pulled me to the shore. Finally I felt firm sand under my feet and staggered onto the beach, coughing and whimpering.

"Franny, Franny," she said, stroking my back gently. "Are you okay? It was only seaweed, Franny. Look, see? Here's some." She held up the strange substance, all green rope with spiky leaves and weird otherworldly growths like tumors, slick and slimy.

"I'm—sorry," I choked, looking at it.

"It was my fault," she said. "I shouldn't have swum so far out."

"I thought—I thought maybe you'd left me…I thought…" I coughed.

"Left you?" She looked at me. "Nah. I—well, I thought about it, swimming out there. Just keep going, you know? Swim to China or something. But nah. I couldn't leave my Franny-Fran."

"Thank you," I said, "for coming back."

She grinned. "There's one problem, though."

"What?"

"I'm freakin' *cold*!"

I giggled. "So am I! Oh, it's *freezing*!"

"Let's get our clothes and get in the van!"

But when we looked, we discovered that we'd left our things too close to the surf: they were all soaked.

"Oh, no! Lucy!"

"Never mind!" she cried. "Just pick 'em up!"

Gasping, shivering with the cold, we gathered them in our arms and ran pell-mell to the vehicle.

"Get in, get in!"

We leapt into the vehicle, slammed the doors shut. We

knocked the sand from our wet feet. There was a little heap of dirty blankets in the back and we each took the end of one, rubbed ourselves dry, our teeth chattering, our skins covered with goose bumps.

After a time we calmed. I reached to the windows around us and closed each set of curtains. We lay back then, pulling one of the dry blankets over ourselves and using another, rolled up, as a pillow.

"I have a couple of shirts in my bag," I said. "They're dry."

"In a bit," Lucy said. "It's too cold to move now."

And it was. But our body heat soon began to warm us, our shoulders pressed together in the narrow space.

"I wish we could hear the *Mystery Theater*," she said after a while.

"Yeah. It's okay like this, though."

"Yeah, it is."

Then she said: "We did it, Franny."

"Yeah. We did."

What would happen later didn't seem to matter then. We were here, together. In our own world. No one on earth could see us or knew where we were. We were happy.

Once we were warmer I asked, "Do you want something to eat? I brought crackers and stuff."

"Okay," she said, looking at me. "Sure. We've been through a lot. We need to build up our strength!"

I smiled, reached over to my rucksack, brought out crackers, bananas, cans of warm Coke. It was the best meal I'd ever eaten. Afterwards Lucy burped loudly. I followed suit. We giggled, goosed each other under the blanket.

"Hey," I said, remembering, rummaging in my bag, "I have my little hairbrush in here." I brought it out, swept it several times through my own hair, then reached to Lucy's.

She turned around and I slowly pulled the brush through hers, untangling the rats' nests as I went. She smelled of the sea; we both did. She grew quiet and calm. Brushing her hair took a long time.

Finally we lay back down together, holding hands. Slowly, wordlessly, we somehow turned to face-to-face, wrapped our arms around each other, the full length of our bodies pressing together. The feeling of another person's skin on mine was strange, thrilling. I found myself looking at her breasts, her hips, awestruck at the idea that, if she wanted to, she could have a baby. And that I would be like that too, soon, even if I couldn't imagine it.

There were several light scars on Lucy's chest, including one across her right breast that ran straight down through the nipple. She saw me looking at it.

"Fran…is it ugly?"

"Lucy, you could never be ugly."

"Honestly?"

Somehow, here, our eyelashes and lips nearly touching, it was okay to say it, to murmur it to her: "I think you're beautiful."

"Aw," she said, "you're a retard."

I found myself touching the scar on her breast, tracing the line gingerly down to her nipple with my index finger, my blood-sister finger.

"Does it hurt?"

"Nah."

"Do you mind my touching it?"

"Nah."

Then I astonished myself. Instinctively, without thinking at all—I never could have done it if I'd thought about it—I leaned down and touched my lips to the top of her breast, where the scar began. Her skin tasted of salt.

She hugged me tightly then. The sensation of her palms on my back, my waist, my thighs sent tiny electric jolts all through me, making me shiver and tingle. Our hands moved. Mine didn't seem under my control at all. We touched each other's faces slowly, gently. I studied her little freckles, the cracked places on her lips. I stroked her shoulders, cupped her breasts in my hands, touched her pubic hair lightly, curiously. Her fingers brushed my chest, my belly, briefly traced over the place between my legs that no one, absolutely no one had ever touched, or, for many years, would again.

"Lucy?" I whispered.

"Hm."

"Lucy, are—are we having sex?"

She snickered. "Franny, you're such a spaz." But then, immediately: "No, I didn't mean that. You're not a spaz at all."

I giggled. Our hands settled again, grew still. Her arm was under my head, the perfect pillow: in my ear I could feel her pulse slowly beating, beating. I sensed that there was something else I should say to her, something more, but in this place, this moment, sleepiness began to overtake me. I could hear the ocean and her heartbeat and after a while there was a light pattering of rain on the roof of the van. Lucy and the sea were all I knew. I drifted away, knowing beyond doubt that the two of us would stay here together forever, even as I knew beyond doubt that they would be coming for us soon. Very soon.

—Eleven—

I DROVE ALL night.
Hey, Mike, how ya doin'?

Well, hey, lovely lady. What brings you here?

Said you'd teach me how to play pool. How 'bout it?

Why, sure, sure! C'mon in!

Where's the pool table?

It's downstairs. C'mon, right through here. Be careful on the steps.

No: it probably didn't happen that way. Lucy would have had no reason to ride her bike out to Mike McCoy's shack that night. She had other plans. But the fact was, no one ever really knew how it *did* happen. McCoy never said, at least not publicly. He never uttered a word during the trial. Apparently he never said anything to his own lawyers. Crucial facts in the timeline of all three cases remained a mystery…Except that they weren't really *crucial facts*. The crucial facts were in that basement. The crucial facts were strewn around the riverbed in pieces.

Hey, lovely lady, whatcha doin' here this time of night?

Hopin' you'll give me a piece of that licorice, Mike.

You bet. Shouldn't you be home, though, this hour?

Nah. It's okay. I got a light on my bike.

Not much business this late. Ain't seen a car come by in an hour. 'Bout to close up.

That's okay.

Hey…if you got nothin' to do, we could shoot some pool.

Really?

Sure.

At your house?

Sure.

No: if it had happened like this, Lucy would have known enough to be suspicious of such an invitation. It must have come from her.

Not much business this late. Ain't seen a car come by in an hour. 'Bout to close up.

That's okay. Hey, maybe we could play pool.

Why, now, that's an idea. Sure. Your mom know where you are, lovely lady?

Nah. I go out like this all the time. She doesn't care.

Well, then, sure. Why don't we toss that bike of yours in the back of my truck?

The bike would be found in the riverbed later.

It was still difficult for me to picture. Would Lucy have been so naïve as to go out to McCoy's isolated shack in the middle of the night—at the very time two girls had been found dead nearby?

Hi, lovely lady.

Mike. Hey, you scared me. Don't sneak up on people like that.

Didn't mean to. Sorry. Whatcha doin' out at this hour of the night?

Nothin'. Thinking about stuff.

Right here on the street corner? This late?

Yeah, well. I dunno.

Better be careful. Pretty girl like you hangin' out on a street corner in the middle of the night…Some guys might get ideas.

What kind of ideas?

You know. Don't tell me you don't know.

Well, maybe I do, maybe I don't.

You do. Pretty girl like you knows a lot, don't you? You know all about things like that.

Hey, Mike, you're acting kind of weird.

Think so?

Yeah.

Well, maybe I'm weird.

Mike, what are you doing?

Don't tell me you don't know what I'm talkin' about, lovely lady.

Mike, hey, c'mon. Let go.

How did he get her in the truck? Did he threaten her? Hit her? Did he knock her unconscious? And the bike: he must have thrown it in the back. What a chance he must have taken, that someone would see it right there in the truck bed. But then they could have seen Lucy, too, in the passenger seat. Unless she was unconscious and shoved down under the line of the window.

I wanted to believe it. I wanted to believe that everything ended for Lucy Sparrow on a street corner in Quiet late one night, ended with a single blow that she never even felt, a blow so hard that her lights went out instantly and forever. I knew she hadn't been dead: she was alive in that basement. That much was known. Alive, yes: but unconscious: blacked-out, unaware. Please, God.

And yet I didn't believe it.

Where are you taking me?

To my house. Remember? I promised we'd shoot some pool together.

Really? That's what we're going to do? Play pool?

Sure. C'mon, lovely lady, relax. We're gonna have us some fun.

It's just that—it's kinda late, you know? Maybe I should just go home.

Nah, c'mon, it's early. Shank of the evenin'.

No, it's late, Mike. My mom will wonder where I am.

It won't take long. Then I'll drive you right back. I'll take you right to your front door.

You promise?

Sure, I promise.

Would she have known then, or suspected? If so, why didn't she jump out of the truck? But it was the middle of the night. The road to his house was a dirt path in the middle of nothingness. And he was an adult, an adult she knew and liked, telling her that she was fine, calling her a lovely lady, assuring her that everything was okay. She was twelve years old; she may even have believed him. After all, despite the warnings we'd heard from the grown-ups in our lives, the story of the recent killings hadn't really permeated our minds; they seemed to have happened in another world, a world of older girls in high school whom we didn't know and who had nothing to do with us.

Sure is dark out here.

Don't worry about it. Nothin' to be afraid of out here.

I'm not afraid of the dark, Mike. I've never been afraid of the dark.

She'd seen the house before; we'd ridden past it on one of our lengthier Saturday-afternoon jaunts. How different it must have looked at night.

C'mon in.

Hey, crazy place you got here, Mike. This is messier than my room.

I'm not much of a housekeeper. Need me a woman to do that. Maybe you could.

Nah. I'm terrible at cleaning things up. I'm the one who makes the messes, not the one who cleans 'em up.

Yeah? I've made a few messes in my life.

I can see, yeah. So where's that pool table?

It's downstairs. Right through here. Careful on the steps.

When would she have realized?

Hey, Mike, it's dark in here.

Well, I'll turn the light on.

Why'd you close the door?

Here's the light switch. Take a look. It's a special place.

I don't see a pool table.

Well, head down the stairs. I'll show you.

What's all this stuff, anyway?

Just some toys I got. Let's play a game.

Mike, I think I'd better leave.

What's your hurry?

What is this thing? This isn't a pool table.

It's a dissecting table. Know what that is? It's where they cut up dead bodies.

Mike, I've got to go. Really. I have to leave. My mom—

Let's play a game, lovely lady.

Mike, the door's locked. Why is the door locked? I have to go home.

C'mere, lovely lady.

I have to go home, Mike.

She would have fought him. He would have been surprised at her strength. Maybe he even complimented her on it.

Wow, you're a tough one! You got some muscles, lovely lady!

She would have tried punching him just as she'd punched Melissa Deaver. She would have clawed at the door. Maybe she screamed; maybe she never had a chance to. What would she have thought as he tore at her clothes, as he hit her again and again so that he could push her up onto the table, strap her down? What did *he* think when he beheld all her scars?

Looks like somebody's been workin' on you already.

Let me go. Please let me go. I won't tell anybody. Really. I promise.

Who did this to you, lovely lady?
Really. I—
I said, who did this to you?
My dad did.

Even Mike McCoy would have been surprised to hear that. Did he hesitate then, even for an instant? Did he think that perhaps he'd chosen the wrong girl? Or did her scars only make her seem that much more right?

They make you look like shit. I thought you were a lovely lady. But you look like shit.

No. Perhaps:

Your dad must be a terrible person, to do something like that to his own daughter. I think that's just awful. But don't worry, kiddo. You're still a lovely lady to me. Really.

Then, even then, would a small part of her have been encouraged by the compliment, would she have sensed a softening in him, had a moment's hope that his sympathy would lead him to release her, apologize, help her with her clothes, drive her back to her house, say gently as she got out of his truck, *Now remember, you promised—this is our little secret, right?*

Sure, Mike. I promise.

When he began his preliminary work with his knives and sharpened screwdrivers, did he carefully avoid her scars? Or did he deliberately seek out each one, open the old wound again, watch it bleed?

Stop. Please stop. It hurts, Mike.
You're a lovely lady. Lovely lady…
It hurts. It hurts, Mike. Oh my God.

But God wasn't listening to Lucy Sparrow that night.
Or perhaps He was.
She'd said to me: *There are just some people that God hates.*
I drove all night.

—Twelve—

M Y CHEEK WAS against Lucy's back when I woke, sometime before dawn. She'd turned over in the night and I was behind her, spooning her, our bodies smoothly interlocked. I peeked out behind one of the van's curtains and saw a deep brown color beginning to glow at the horizon, far off. It was still dark but the sun was coming, I knew. We had to decide what we were going to do, where we would go. And I had a fierce need to go to the bathroom.

I shook her gently. "Lucy?"

"Go 'way," she muttered.

"Lucy, wake up."

"Mmm…why?"

"Because the sun is coming up soon. We can't just stay here."

I saw her eyes open slowly. She sniffed, swallowed, cleared her throat. "Yeah," she said. "You're probably right." Turning over toward me, she pushed the blanket away.

"Lucy, I have to pee."

"So, go."

"I can't go like *this.*"

"Well, put your clothes on, then."

"But it's still dark out there."

"Oh." She didn't make fun of me. She just said, "Okay."

Silently we sorted through our clothing. I took out the fresh things I'd brought and Lucy put on one of my shirts; it was too small for her, but at least it was dry. Our pants and shoes were still damp, but there was nothing to be done about

163

it; we slipped into them. My eyes stung, my mouth tasted bad. My neck still throbbed slightly from the accident. My shoulder hurt from sleeping on the hard floor.

Finally we emerged from the van, the predawn breeze cold in our faces.

"Do you think we can still drive it?" I asked, looking at the big dent at the back of the vehicle. One of the taillights had been crushed.

"We don't have any gas, Fran. Remember?"

"Well," I said, "what are we going to do? We can't stay here. People are bound to come soon. The person who owns this snack booth will come."

"How do I know what we're gonna do? You think of something. You're smart."

"Well—I have to *go* first," I said.

"Yeah. So do I, actually. Do we have any toilet paper?"

I shook my head. "I've got a couple of paper napkins."

"Well, that'll have to do."

We tromped through the sand, toward one of the ominous-looking dunes. When I looked back I realized that I couldn't see the van anymore. I was suddenly frightened and took Lucy's hand.

"It's okay, Fran," she said.

We found a place. I gave her one of the napkins. When each of us was finished we stood and zipped up. But as we moved toward the van again I thought I heard a faint sound.

"Lucy—wait. Listen."

We stood completely still. The ocean rumbled. For a moment I wasn't sure; then I was. It was a car.

We looked at each other. Then we hustled behind a small pile of sand, a kind of mini-dune. We peered up over the top.

There was a pickup truck pulling into the parking lot. It drove straight over to the snack stand, stopped, and a Hispanic-looking man with a mustache got out. He looked at the van, looked at the side of his building.

"Shit," we heard him say.

He moved to the van, to *our* van. He studied the damage in the rear and then peered through the windows. Then he looked around quizzically. We saw him shake his head. He moved to the little stand then, unlocked the door at the rear. We could see him standing in there in the darkness, picking up a phone.

"Crap," Lucy said. "He's calling the cops, I bet."

"Maybe we could make a run for it," I suggested. "Jump into the van and take off before he knows what's happening. We must have enough gas to get us a *little* ways."

"Then what?" She dropped down behind the little dune. We hid against the wall of sand. "No, we need to get farther away. Up there." She pointed to a larger dune somewhat further back which had some scrubby bushes at its top. She grabbed my hand. "C'mon, while he's in there!"

We ran, the sand sucking at our shoes. I was out of breath by the time we reached the dune, ran around to its far side, and began climbing it. Finally we reached the top, peered over between the bushes.

In a few minutes a police car rolled into the parking lot. I'd thought it might come at top speed, with lights flashing and siren blaring, but it didn't. It pulled easily up to the snack shack and a big cop got out. The Hispanic-looking man greeted him. The breeze took their words, but it was obvious what they were saying to each other as they looked at the damage to the building, looked at the van. The cop surveyed the area carefully, as if through his sheer power of vision he would root out the evildoers.

We dropped behind the dune.

"What now?" I asked, shaking sand out of my shoes. I

was thirsty.

"Maybe," she said, "we could head off past the dunes into those hills." She pointed.

I looked. "And go where? Do you know where we are?"

"No," she admitted. "Not really."

We sat there glumly. We could hear the cop's car radio squawking as he spoke into it. Dawn began to glow on the horizon, past the dunes. The brown sky slowly turned a deep red and then began to lighten to a soft pink. Soon it was morning, a beautiful early-spring morning. We didn't move except to brush sand off ourselves and to occasionally look over the rise of the dune. I wished we could go walking on the beach, barefoot, splashing each other with the water. I wished we could walk up to the snack bar and ask the man for two hot dogs and two ice-cold Cokes. I wished we could punch the tetherball at each other at Soames Elementary. I wished we could do anything but sit here motionlessly, waiting for doom to come.

"What are we going to *do*, Lucy?"

"I *don't know.* Stop asking me."

After a time there was the sound of more cars coming into the parking lot: another police car and a car I recognized immediately. It belonged to Frank and Louise.

"Oh my God," I whispered. "Look."

We looked. Two cops were in the police car, but we hardly noticed them. Instead we both watched the other car as it pulled in and Frank and Louise stepped out of the front. Ms. Sparrow came out from the back.

"Oh crap," Lucy whispered.

Again we watched the discussion in pantomime: showing them the van, looking inside (we hadn't locked the doors—they just opened it and looked, which made me feel somehow abused, *violated*), studying the damage at the back and on the building. When the breeze changed direction we could hear scraps of their words: *Where did they. How. Must be around. Run away?*

"Frances?" my aunt called. *"Frances!"*

"Lucy?" shouted Ms. Sparrow. "Where are you, Punk? *Lucy?"*

"Frances! *Frances!"*

Everyone there peered in different directions, stepping tentatively this way and that. The cops joined in: *"Lucy? Frances?"* called their rough, unfamiliar voices.

After a minute or two of this they gathered together again. I saw one of the cops gesturing down toward the beach and two of them moved off toward the shore. The rest stood there talking. *Haven't gone far. Couldn't just. Stuff still here.*

The sun rose in the sky, bright and hot on my face. A headache had begun to pulse behind my eyes. I was itchy and sore, hungry and thirsty. Lucy sat close to me, morose, not meeting my eyes. At last, frustrated, frightened, I started to cry.

"Aw, crap," Lucy said disgustedly. "Fran, shut the hell up."

"*You* shut up. You're the one who got us into this."

"Nobody forced you to come."

"You said we were going to Malibu. To *Hollywood.*"

"Yeah, well, that didn't work out, did it? Sorry. Excuse me for *living.*"

"Lucy," I said through my tears, "we have to give up. You know we do."

"Give up, nothin'. We can hide in these dunes for a long time."

"And eat what? And drink what? Where do we go when it rains?"

She chuckled sadly. "Maybe we'll find a cave."

I chuckled too. I would have loved to find a cave to stay in with Lucy. Just to stay there together, forever and ever.

"Just…stop crying, okay?" she said.

I wiped my eyes. "I'm sorry."

"Maybe," she said flatly, "you shouldn't have thrown away my razor. You know?"

I glanced at her. "Maybe."

"Do you think," she asked, a speculative look in her eyes, "they'll let us go home?"

"I don't know. We stole a *car*. And we wrecked it."

"Yeah, but we're, like, little kids. We're not even teenagers. Well, I *almost* am."

"I don't know, Lucy." Home or jail cell or cold dank dungeon, I wanted to say, I didn't care, as long as we could be together. But we had to leave here.

"Okay," she sighed.

It was mid-morning, the sun high in the sky now. We stood.

"I'm afraid," I said.

"Don't be. It'll be okay."

I sniffed, nearly began crying again, but managed to hold it back.

"Lucy—"

"Look," she said impatiently, "if we're gonna go, let's *go,* okay?"

I swallowed, nodded. "Okay."

With that, we climbed down the dune and walked, separately, hands in pockets, toward the waiting cars.

We weren't allowed to go home—at least not right away. In fact, we were arrested, and for a few moments one of the cops dangled a deadly-looking pair of handcuffs in front of my eyes. They glinted in the morning sun, terrifying me, yet, staring at them, I couldn't help but wonder if they could actually hold my wrists. They were so big that it looked as if they might fall off completely.

No one really seemed to know how to proceed. There was talk of putting us in one of the police cruisers, but Ms. Sparrow said, "For God's sake, officers, we can take them to the station in our car. These aren't hardened criminals here."

Discussion. Much radio communication. At last it was agreed that we would follow the police cruiser directly to the station.

Lucy and Ms. Sparrow sat in the back; I was in front, between Frank and Louise. The drive was slow, miserable, like a funeral procession. Not a single word was spoken during the ride. I hoped I wouldn't start crying, and I didn't. What was happening seemed bigger than tears.

Lucy and I were put into a waiting room at the station while the adults in our lives went off to talk to the police. I could hear Ms. Sparrow's raised voice at one point, though I couldn't make out the words. Lucy and I sat on either end of a long wooden bench. There was a policewoman sitting just outside the doorway, at a desk, but no one else was actually in the room with us. Yet somehow it seemed impossible to slide over to Lucy now, to whisper in her ear, to gossip or giggle or to do so much as to say a word. We didn't even look at each other. It felt as if we'd been caught doing something dirty, not simply committing a wrong like taking a van for a joyride (I learned the word "joyride" by overhearing some cops talking in the corridor). I didn't feel like a criminal, but I felt embarrassed, ashamed of myself, as I had once when Lucy and I had gazed at the copy of *Playgirl* in the toilet stall. I wanted to take a bath.

I don't know how long we were left there. It seemed like

hours. Will they put us in a jail cell? I wondered. Will we be separate or together? Will other people be in there—grown-up rapists, murderers? Will we get food? What if I have to to go to the bathroom—do they have bathrooms in jail cells? When will they let us out? Will there be a trial, like on the old *Perry Mason* TV show? Will lawyers put us on the stand and shout at us, try to break us down, admit our crimes? Will we turn on each other then, like criminals in movies always do?

Lucy talked me into it, Your Honor. I didn't want to do it.

No, it was Fran's idea. I only did the driving 'cuz I knew how. Hell, she was the one who shifted it into third.

She had a razor, Your Honor. I was scared.

Fran would always cry if she didn't get her way. I knew what we were doing was wrong, Mr. Judge, but I felt sorry for her—I mean, look at her. She's such a spaz.

No: no, we couldn't, mustn't. We couldn't lie about each other or accuse each other. We'd done it together; we both knew that. We had to tell the truth, face whatever happened together. We were blood sisters, after all.

I looked over at her. She was leaning forward, hands clasped before her, staring at the floor. Her hair obscured her face.

"Lucy?"

She didn't look at me. "What?"

"Lucy, I—"

Just then fast footsteps came up the corridor and we both turned. Ms. Sparrow appeared before the policewoman's desk, spoke to her briefly. Then the policewoman looked back into the room where Lucy and I were seated.

"Lucille Sparrow!" she called.

Lucy jumped up and moved to the corridor. I could see her talking to her mother, but couldn't hear their words. A moment later I saw Frank and Louise. The policewoman looked back into the room again.

"Frances Pastan!"

I walked toward the doorway. My uncle was signing some papers. Lucy stood with her back to me, not speaking. We all rode home together in perfect silence.

I'd feared that the storm would burst when I was alone with my aunt and uncle in the house, but it didn't. In fact, at first, nothing happened at all.

"Go to your room, Frances," my aunt instructed.

I did. It was mid-afternoon; the sun was shining through my window. I saw that they had replaced the window screen which I'd removed the night before—but was it really only the night before? It seemed months, years. I felt as if I'd stepped over a threshold, that the person I'd been before was only a little girl; now I was something different. What, I didn't know. I wasn't a grown-up. I wasn't even a teenager. But I wasn't the same as I'd been.

For hours the house was tomb-like in its silence, a silence finally broken by the low-volume game shows Aunt Louise always watched in the afternoon. I thought I could smell, very faintly, the odor of her Marlboro cigarette. I lay on my bed, hands clasped behind my head, staring at the ceiling. Something had to happen, I knew. Sooner or later. I was hungry; luckily I'd brought my rucksack with me from the van and found it still held a stray banana. I ate it.

Strange. Alone in my room, I no longer felt the embarrassment I'd suffered around the grown-ups. I felt no shame at all at what we'd done. If anything, I sensed within me a certain pride: we'd done something other kids our age couldn't even dream of. We were wild, crazy. We were rebels. I smiled at the thought, a thrill coursing through me. Where was the bland, obedient, meek little Frances Pastan now? She'd disappeared, gotten lost somewhere between the moment I met Lucy and the moment we surrendered ourselves to the police. I would never be the same, I knew. Not that I had any intention of becoming a car thief or a criminal of any sort; but what Lucy and I had gone through had changed me, turned me into something else, something more than I'd been.

Still, I knew that what had happened was serious— that it was going to have serious repercussions. And then I remembered what had set the events in motion in the first place: the fact that Lucy was moving away. I'd not thought of it for the entire time we'd been in the van. Moving. *Leaving me.*

No. Surely her mother would reconsider. She would see what we were to each other. She would know that it would be disastrous to rip Lucy away from her closest friend ever, her best friend. The police could be alerted about Lucy's father, surely. No, Ms. Sparrow couldn't take Lucy away. She *couldn't.*

But I saw another side to it, too. Lucy had been in trouble before, but nothing like this. I could see it the way her mother might: how that little Pastan girl who looked so innocent and acted so shy had really been pulling her daughter in a bad direction. Well, maybe not pulling, exactly: surely Ms. Sparrow couldn't believe that I was some sort of evil influence. But she would see that the two of us together did things that either of us apart would never have done. Would Lucy have broken Melissa's nose if I hadn't been there to protect? Would she have driven a stolen car all the way to the beach by herself? No. It was the two of us together who were causing all the problems.

That was how she would see it.

It was certainly how my aunt and uncle saw it, I thought. I knew my aunt's opinion of the Sparrows, of Lucy. I could almost hear her now: *That damned butch tomboy is who did it. She twisted Frances's mind. It's that Sparrow girl that's to blame.*

I heard raised voices in the other room. My aunt was on the phone to someone; I couldn't make out who. It might have been Ms. Sparrow; perhaps they were hurling accusations at each other. Only a few words reached me behind the closed door to my room. *Damage. Pay. Blame.*

Then, later—the sun was setting by now—there was another conversation, a quieter one. It was my uncle this time, his voice low as always, gentle. I pressed my ear to the crack between my door and the doorframe, where I could hear the best. The sound was still fragmentary, but I could hear some of what he said.

Stole a car. Friend of hers. Police.

Long silence.

No, not. Frances. Car.

Long silence.

Decided. Can't. Too wild.

Long silence.

Have to send home. Check schedules.

I felt myself sliding down to the floor. My breath was short.

They were sending me back to my parents.

The world went black.

When I was awakened by a knock at my window, I wasn't surprised.

It was dark; long past midnight. My aunt and uncle had gone to bed hours before. Neither had said a word to me all afternoon and evening, and I hadn't left my room except to go to the bathroom. Around six my aunt had brought in a tray with a hamburger patty, some green beans, and a little pile of

Tater Tots along with a glass of milk. She didn't look at me. She placed the tray on my desk silently, turned and walked out, closing the door quietly behind her.

I surprised myself with my hunger. I'd thought I would leave the food there untouched, but the smell of the Tater Tots (a favorite) overwhelmed my resistance. I would eat just one, I decided. Then I decided that I would eat the potatoes but nothing else. Finally I gave in, cleaned the plate, drank down all the milk. After all, I hadn't had a real meal since dinner the night before.

I put the tray outside my door. Later I heard someone come and pick it up, take it away.

My mind seemed empty of thought. I let the room grow dark, not bothering to turn on the lights. When it was time for the *Mystery Theater* I turned it on, but only listened to it for a few minutes. It didn't seem right, somehow, here, now, by myself. I switched it off. The room was silent then.

Finally, clicking on my little desk lamp, I looked at what I'd been working on the evening before: the things Lucy and I had planned to put in our time capsule. I had them all there before me. A photo of each of us. A map of the town (in thirty years we wanted to see if it would be different, or exactly the same). Pictures clipped from Lucy's magazines (I was only to be allowed one of Donny Osmond, while Lucy got six of John Travolta). A couple of newspaper headlines. And our drawings. I hadn't yet seen Lucy's, but mine was in progress: a multicolored sketch of the two of us floating in the air, all smiles, Lucy in her Bachman-Turner Overdrive T-shirt and I in my favorite sloppy yellow sweater. Both of us had angels' wings sprouting from our backs. Yet the picture was drawn realistically, not in a satirical or cartoonish way; I thought it was my best ever. I'd considered asking Uncle Frank if I could somehow get it copied, maybe even in color; I wanted to give one to Lucy which I would sign in the corner, *For Lucy, With All My Love, Franny-Fran.*

But the picture was still unfinished, only half colored-in with the artist's pencils I liked to use. I took one of them up now, started desultorily to fill in some of the background; but I couldn't focus on it. I put the pencil down again, switched off the lamp, dropped back onto my bed and stared into nothingness. Everything was wrong now. Everything was flying apart even as I lay there. Grown-ups were deciding things about me, about Lucy. They would determine where we would live and with whom and who we would see and wouldn't see. Yet the people who were making the decisions knew nothing about me, about us.

I had a fantasy then, about Lucy and me living together in an apartment somewhere. It was a beautiful place with hanging plants everywhere and my pictures lining the walls. There was a sunroof in the middle of the living room that opened straight to the sky and we would sunbathe there in the mornings. We would make meals together, big ones, with everything we liked and nothing we didn't. On nice days we would go outside, play football on the big lawn in front, chase each other, climb trees. At night we would listen to the radio and sleep cuddled together in a great big bed. There was no one else in the fantasy. No parents, no aunts or uncles, no teachers, no neighbors, no classmates. It was a world of two, complete, unassailable.

I must have fallen asleep, for it was dark when the knocking on the window woke me. My curtains weren't closed; as soon as I turned to the window I saw her there.

I went to the door, made sure my aunt and uncle had gone to bed, and then opened the window, the screen between us.

We didn't say anything or even look at each other for a while. Finally Lucy whispered, "Are you in trouble?"

"Sure I'm in trouble. What did you think? I wasn't allowed out of my room all day."

"Yeah," she said. "Me neither." She stood there awkwardly. "So, you grounded?"

"Lucy," I said, "they're going to send me back to my parents. In Fresno."

She looked at me. "I bet they won't, Fran. They're probably just mad—"

"No," I said. "My uncle called them. They've got it all arranged."

"When do you go?"

I shook my head. "I don't know. They haven't told me."

Silence.

"Are you still moving too?"

"Yeah," she said. "At least I think so. I heard my mom on the phone to some people earlier."

I leaned my forehead against the screen. I felt utterly empty, defeated.

"Did you listen to the *Mystery Theater*?" I asked finally.

"Nah."

"Neither did I. I tried, but it wasn't the same."

"I know."

Silence.

"Have you finished your picture?" I asked.

"Picture?"

"For the time capsule."

"Oh." She shook her head. "No. I started one, with hearts and stuff in it. But…crap, Fran, I can't draw anyway. You should do it."

"I am," I said. "But it was supposed to be both of us."

"Yeah. I dunno."

I moved to my desk, picked up my own unfinished drawing, held it to the screen.

"Oh my God," Lucy breathed. "Fran, that's really good. I mean that's *really* good. It's beautiful."

"Thanks," I smiled wearily. "It's not finished yet. I have to fill in all the color. But…" I put the picture down again. "I don't know. Maybe I'll never finish it."

"You should. It's great. Really."

Silence.

"Franny, I—I kinda wish you'd cry or something. It's weird, you just standing there like that, looking at me."

"I'm done crying," I said. "I don't want to cry anymore. I'm too tired to cry."

She stood there in the darkness, her hair haloed by the moonlight.

How had I gotten here? I wondered. In this house? In this town? This wasn't where I was supposed to be. I should never have known anything at all in my life about Quiet, California, or Lucy Sparrow, or anything.

Why do I have to go, Dad?
Mom, what did I do?

"Hey, Franny…I got my bike."

"What?"

"I got my bike. We could go."

"Go where?"

"I dunno. Maybe we could find that cave we were talking about."

"Oh, Lucy. There's no cave."

"Sure there are. In the mountains. We could find one."

"That's crazy, Lucy."

"No, this time we'd take food. A lot of it. We could hide out. We could survive a long time."

"No, we couldn't."

"Fran, really. C'mon. Okay, so maybe not a cave. We could ride out to the freeway and hitchhike."

"In the middle of the night?"

"Why not? There're cars."

"Cars that would pick up two twelve-year-old girls? What kind of cars would those be?"

"I'm almost thirteen."

"You're *twelve.*"

She stood there for a moment.

"Well, crap, Fran, you don't have to get mad."

"I'm not mad," I sighed. "I'm not anything."

"We could ride out to the ocean."

"Lucy, the ocean is twenty or thirty miles away."

"I'm strong."

"Not that strong. And even if you were, they'd catch us. It would be tomorrow by the time we got there. They'd catch us, Lucy. They'd always catch us, no matter where we went."

A flash of annoyance crossed her features. "I thought we were blood sisters."

"We are."

"Then c'mon. Come with me."

"Lucy, no."

"We've got the whole night. We can get away someplace."

"No. We can't."

She stared at me, her silver-gray eyes sparkling in the darkness.

"I don't wanna go alone, Franny-Fran."

"You shouldn't go at all. You should just go home. That's where you should go."

"Crap."

"Or you could come in here, Lucy. Spend the night with me. We'd get in trouble in the morning, but it's better than going out there in the dark."

"That wouldn't get us away from here."

"No," I admitted. "It wouldn't."

"C'mon, Franny-Fran. Come on out. We'll go someplace. Together!"

I wondered if I would cry, but no. What I felt was deeper than tears.

"No, Lucy."

"Come *on.*"

"No. You should go home, Lucy. Get some sleep."

"I don't want to. I want you to come out with me."

"I can't. You can come in here if you want. It's okay. I'll open the screen."

"We need to get *away,* Franny."

"No."

She looked at me, her face tight with perplexity.

"No?" she said. "Really? No?"

"No," I whispered.

We looked at each other. After a while I placed my palm on the window screen. She did the same. I could feel the pressure of her hand pushing against mine.

Then she moved away. "You're not gonna rat on me, are you, Fran?"

"Lucy, just go home. Go *home.*"

She sighed. "Okay."

"Really? You will?"

"Sure. Stupid idea anyway."

"Go home, Lucy. Go to sleep. Maybe things will look different in the morning."

"Maybe."

"Maybe we can—maybe they'll let us see each other. Or maybe we can talk on the phone."

"Yeah."

"And we'll write to each other. Wherever we are. Long letters."

"Sure."

"And then, when we're older—" I felt my voice breaking, my life breaking. "When we're older we'll…we'll…"

"Sure, Franny-Fran." She began to move off, the night swallowing her.

"You're going home, Lucy? Really?"

"Yeah. 'Bye, Fran."

"'Bye, Lucy."

She disappeared into the darkness.

The next morning, quite early—it was still dark—Aunt Louise came in with two big suitcases and slowly began folding my things into them. She didn't tell me why. I didn't need to ask.

"I can do that, Aunt Louise."

She glanced at me. "It's all right," she said. She kept folding. "You be ready in an hour, okay? Frank will drive you to the station and see that you get on the bus all right."

"Okay. I'm—I'm sorry, Aunt Louise."

She didn't reply. It took only a few minutes to pack my things. She left.

I didn't see her again. I saw only my uncle, grim-faced. He helped me put my bags in the car.

Standing there in the driveway, moments from leaving Quiet, California forever—or at least for the next thirty years—I looked over at the Sparrows' house. It was silent and still in the unknowing dawn.

—Thirteen—

IT TOOK ME one week to find him.

Driving across the Mojave Desert one sees little but an endless canvas of white, broken occasionally by indistinct blurs of tan or beige or ochre. Joshua trees, sage, and cactus predominate, when there's anything living at all. It's then, at midday, with no live thing in one's range of vision, no cars in sight, that it seems as if what one is really traversing is the bright side of the moon. It's almost impossible to imagine that the air outside the car windows is breathable, and indeed, it hardly is: the heat gives it a thickness that's stubbornly difficult to pull into human lungs. The ribbon of road stretches into the glaring distance farther than one can see, seemingly forever.

Yet eventually, rising like some garish phoenix out of the ashes, comes civilization, or at least Las Vegas—that most unnatural of cities. I'd been here once as a college girl, on a senior trip with friends; I remembered the basic layout of the place, the creepy timelessness of the never-closing bars and casinos, the cheap and vulgar tone of it all, the way that, up close, everything seemed smaller than it should have been, and dirtier.

And yet I'd enjoyed it then; I enjoyed it now, after the newspaper offices and libraries were closed, once there was really nothing more I could do that day. I spent too much money, as one always does in Las Vegas. I played slots and poker. I socialized with boozy salesmen from Oklahoma, overweight executives from Chicago, and nervous college boys from Connecticut, one of whom came to my room one night

181

and left, of course, before the next morning.

I wasted time, I wasted money. But in the end I found him.

As it turned out, he didn't really live in Las Vegas, or if he did, it was at the very limit of the town. It was a long drive on a road white with desert dust, past all houses, all businesses, any signs of life. I was sure I'd taken a wrong turn; there was nothing out here but sun, sky, small hills in the distance. And yet, finally, quite literally at the end of the road, I saw a wooden shack.

It was truly a shack. Warped, dilapidated, the sight of it reminded me of nothing so much as period photographs of the Depression. It had a single window in the front, gray with grime. There was an old car parked beside the structure, but it didn't look drivable. It was as if the desert were about to swallow this place, push it down with its winds, bury it in its sands. At first I couldn't believe that anybody really lived here; surely it had been abandoned years before.

And yet as I sat in my air-conditioned car looking at the place, the door was pulled open. I knew then that I was in the wrong location, for out stepped an old man wearing thick horn-rimmed glasses and a plain blue work shirt and jeans. His sparse hair was white, stringy, sprouting in different directions on his head. He was stooped over to an extent that it appeared as if he had a hump on his back; his head, as he moved, tilted down at a precarious angle. His mouth was perpetually open and I could see a line of suspiciously full and even teeth: surely dentures. He'd seen me, or heard me; it couldn't have been difficult, out here in the desert silence. He looked at me, head facing down, eyes looking up under his white and overgrown eyebrows.

I was about to put the car in gear, perhaps mouth the word *Sorry* as I pulled away, but he waved to me. His arm moved unnaturally, jerkily, like a marionette's. He seemed to be smiling, but in that ancient face it was hard to tell: he might just have been squinting his eyes in the brightness.

I rolled my window down a crack. The furnace-air hit my eyes, made them water.

"Got my groceries?" he called from across the street, his voice high and wheezy, as if with each word he somehow leaked air.

"Your…? No, I'm sorry. I think I made a wrong turn."

He looked at me, mouth hanging. His skin was hard, leathery, nearly mummified. It seemed pasted to his bones, as if there were nothing underneath it at all: no muscle, no fat. I couldn't even imagine how old this man must be, or how long he had left to live.

"Wrong turn?" he called. "Where you goin'?"

I rolled the window down a bit further, felt my face burst into a sweat almost instantly. "I'm looking for a Mike Jones," I said, giving the name I'd been told he used now, had been using for the past decade since he'd been free.

The man smiled then—it truly was a smile, I saw his mouth curve crookedly upward—and walked toward my car.

"I'm Mike Jones," he rasped.

I stared at him as he shuffled toward me, becoming ever larger in my field of vision. It was impossible, I realized; I'd been given bad information. He came up to me and I said, "Well, I think I have the wrong person. It must be a different Mike Jones I'm looking for. I'm sorry to have bothered you."

"Well," he said, "don't gotta be in a rush. Have some water before you go."

"Oh, thank you, Mr. Jones, but I'm okay." I held up the bottle of water that I'd been slowly sipping for hours.

"Um." He was visibly disappointed. Part of his face, I saw, seemed frozen, or if not frozen, at least stiffened, difficult to move. That was why his smile was crooked. Stroke, I realized.

I was at a dead end, it seemed—literally and figuratively. My head hurt from the desert heat as well as from the liberal amount of drinking I'd been doing since I hit Vegas. Like most alcoholics, I never had hangovers; but I still could find myself feeling tired and achy after a night's indulgence. The memory of the college student who'd leapt so enthusiastically into my hotel bed, only to crawl out again under cover of darkness, didn't help. I wondered what it took to find a man who wouldn't be ashamed to look at me when he woke in the morning. Of course, in truth, I disliked looking at myself in the morning too.

"Well, Mr. Jones, it's been nice talking to you—"

"Young lady," he said, "would you do me a favor?"

I looked at him. "What's that?"

He licked his cracked lips. "Well, fact is, the woman who's supposed to bring my groceries ain't showed up. Thought she was due yesterday, but I ain't seen her. Don't know where she is."

"Can't you call her?"

"Ain't got a phone, young lady. Just live out here by myself."

"You have a car."

"That thing? That thing ain't run in five years. I can't drive no more, anyway. Can't see nothin'."

"Well, I'm sorry, but…"

"What I mean is, could you give me a ride to the store?"

I looked at him. He was quivering, I realized; Parkinson's, or something like it. The veins on the backs of his hands were dark and jagged against the liver spots on his skin.

"Well, I—Mr. Jones—"

"Sure be a help," he said. "Don't know what happened to her. She's always so reliable. Unless," he said, "you're in a hurry."

"Well, yes, I—I am."

He nodded. "Okay, then. Sorry to bother you. Have a nice day." And with that he turned, very slowly, and began making his way to the shack again.

I watched him. Finally I called, "Mr. Jones?"

He turned. "Yeah?"

"Where—where is the store?"

He shuffled toward me again, stopped halfway in the road. He pointed. "There's a little place over yonder," he said. "'Bout two miles. Dirt track. Your car'd be okay."

I frowned, but knew I would be consumed with guilt if I left this ancient man with no help at all. I studied him: he was truly no threat. He was a man who was about to die.

"Well—you're sure it's two miles?"

"Positive."

I sighed. "Well—I guess. All right."

He smiled again. "Let me get my money, okay?"

"Yes, sure."

He moved off, noticeably more energetic now. I rolled up my window, unlocked the passenger door. I pulled the car around so that he would be able to step straight out of his front door into the vehicle without crossing the road.

"Hey, thanks," he said when he appeared again. He stepped gingerly in.

"Now," I said, "you have to give me directions."

He did. We drove for perhaps a mile back the way I'd come, then took a dusty fork in the road I'd not even noticed before. It belatedly occurred to me that I might have offered him the use of my cell phone to call the person he was expecting, but by this point it was too late. Another mile or so brought us to a tiny brick building: the store. I went in with him. The place was old, perhaps as old as he was. Native American rugs and geegaws were everywhere, along with a small selection of groceries. I held a basket for him as he picked up bread, coffee, beef jerky, cans of beer. As we reached the counter the proprietor, a pale heavyset man in a T-shirt who looked nothing like a Native American, greeted him in a friendly way: "Nice to see you, Mr. Jones," he said, ringing up the purchases. He glanced at me, smiling. "Ma'am."

"Hello."

"Mr. Jones, is this Eloise's replacement?"

"Hah?"

"Eloise. Is this lady her replacement? Is she helping you now?"

He shook his head. "Don't know nothin' 'bout no replacement."

"Sure you do, Mr. Jones," the proprietor said. "Eloise was moving, remember? You were supposed to call the—"

Mr. Jones looked up. "I forgot," he said wheezily. "By damn, I forgot all about that."

"Forgot?" The proprietor looked genuinely concerned. "Hey, Mr. Jones, you'd better use our phone here. Call them, get her replacement lined up."

"Yeah," he agreed, paying. "Yeah, I'd better do that."

The proprietor produced a phone, handed the receiver to Mr. Jones. "Do you remember the number?"

"I—no. No, I don't think I do. Got it written down, but that's back at the house."

"Well, then, you just call the Operator." The proprietor punched the zero.

While Mr. Jones took care of his business, the proprietor looked at me. Before he asked I said, "I just happened to take a wrong turn onto his road. I don't even know him."

"Well," he said, "you did your good deed for the day. Old Mr. Jones is kind of feeble these days." Then, more quietly,

"Likely to die out in that shack sometime."

I nodded. After a few minutes the old man concluded his business, and we headed back up the road.

When it hit me it really wasn't a surprise; I guess part of me had realized it all along. But it was only when he offered me a piece of jerky, saying, "I really ought to give you somethin' to eat, lovely lady like you," that I admitted to myself that this man was, of course, Mike McCoy. Through the wheezing, air-filled sound of his aged voice, the words *lovely lady*—their tone, their inflection—were unmistakable.

We pulled up to his shack.

"Wanna come in?" he asked.

I looked at him closely, this harmless old desert rat.

"All right," I said. "I'll come in."

He was delighted, his crooked grin bursting forth. We got out of the car.

"Ain't had a visitor in a long time," he said, "other than those people who bring my groceries. An' they never stop to chat."

"That's too bad," I said.

The shack was a single dark room. An oil lamp sat on the table. The shack was only slightly cooler than outside; I was sweating through my shirt.

"You don't have electricity?" I asked.

"Nah. Got a propane tank out back. Keeps my hot plate goin'. Fan, when I need it. Sit down, sit down," he said.

I did. We positioned ourselves at opposite ends of the single table. In the far corner of the room was an old bed, rumpled and sagging. There was a shelf that held a few knick knacks, a shortwave radio, the aforementioned fan, a few miscellaneous magazines.

"Ain't much," he admitted, noticing me looking around.

"No," I agreed.

"All I need now, though. I'm eighty-one years old. Don't need a lot."

"No."

We sat in silence. He popped open one of the beers he'd bought at the store. I declined his offer of one.

"Like to drink 'em when they're still cold," he explained. "No fridge."

"I see that."

"Ain't had a visitor in a long time," he said. "I told you that, didn't I?"

"Yes. You did."

Lucy, just go home.

"Forget a lotta things now," he said quietly. His held his beer in two hands and yet it still quivered as it made its way to his lips.

"Do you?"

"I'm an old man," he said. His voice was breathy, a hall of whispers. "Remember things that happened when I was little. Remember a dog I had, golden retriever. Bucky. Named him after Captain America's sidekick." He grinned crookedly. "Remember a lot of things like that. Way back. But lots is gone. Just disappeared. When they had me in that place they did things to me. Don't recall exactly what. Bright lights, like a burnin' in my head. They were gonna burn out the bad stuff, they said. Don't know what that was. I just recall the burnin', the burnin'. Brighter in my head than that desert out there."

"Do you remember," I said, my breath short, "Lucy Sparrow?"

"What's that?"

"Lucy. Sparrow. Do you remember her?"

"Who's that?"

"Or Maria Sanchez? Or Trista Blake?"

"Is one of them the lady that's supposed to bring my

groceries?"

I looked at him. His eyes were distorted behind the big glasses. He wasn't lying, wasn't pretending, unless he was the greatest actor of all time.

"Your name isn't Jones," I said. "It's McCoy. Mike McCoy. And those are the girls you killed."

"What's that?"

"Lucy Sparrow. The other two. You killed them. You took them down to your basement and you tortured them and you murdered them."

His face looked concerned, confused. "I did?"

"You did."

He shook his head. "You know, I kind of think—it's like there's stuff buried back there, stuff that wasn't totally burned out—it's—but I can't imagine. Why would I do that?"

"I was hoping," I said, "that you would tell me." My throat was dry. I'd been in this shack for five or ten minutes but it felt like hours, hours of roasting hell.

"I don't," he said, shaking his head, "I don't remember none of that."

"Think," I said. "Lucy Sparrow. A big blonde girl. She wore T-shirts and blue jeans. You met her at the Red Ball gas station where you worked. You met me there, too."

"We know each other?"

"I was Lucy's best friend."

He shook his head again, face concentrated with thought. "Can't remember nobody named Lucy."

"You must remember your basement," I said. "Your basement in Quiet, California. Your tools. Your dissecting table. You must remember killing those girls and hacking their bodies up with your bone saw and dropping their—their *parts* in the riverbed. *You must remember that.*"

He looked frightened now. I realized suddenly that I'd

stood up, was leaning across the table, looming over him. He recoiled, his expression suffused with fear. He said nothing. His mouth hung open. He quivered.

I strode away from the table, the heat causing my head to pulsate. I marched to the shelf and lashed out, knocking the magazines everywhere and sending the radio skittering across the floor. There was a small kitchen area where he stored his food and I saw a butcher knife there. I grabbed it, turned to face him.

"Do you remember what you did?" I said. "Do you?"

He couldn't speak. His face had gone an ashy white. I walked up to him, stood there with the knife in my hands.

How's it hangin', lovely ladies?

You girls like to shoot pool?

C'mon over. We'll have us some fun.

"Where's your pool table?" I said.

"What?" he whispered.

"Pool. Pool. Don't you like to play pool?"

"Ain't shot pool in years."

"How about girls? Have you hacked up any girls?"

"Ain't—ain't shot pool in years. The other—it's—"

"It's *what*?"

"It's—ma'am, what kind of a man would do those things? It's nothin' a decent man would do."

I looked at him for a long time. His dark eyes began to seem familiar behind the glasses: the broken blood vessels, the heavy old lids. But the energy in me dissipated then. I dropped the knife, collapsed in the chair next to him.

"Ain't sayin'," he murmured, "ain't sayin' I didn't do it. Maybe I did. I heard about this before. There were people before came here. Maybe I did do it. Guess I'll—guess I'll go to hell if I did. Guess that's where I belong. It sounds like an awful thing, a terrible thing. But ma'am, I don't know what you're talkin' about. I don't remember nothin' from back then. Only remember ol' Bucky. Did I tell you about Bucky?"

"Yes," I whispered, "you did."

"Bucky was my golden retriever." He was proud of this, of remembering this. "Named him after Captain America's sidekick. Bucky. Beautiful dog. We used to swim together in the creek in the summers."

I stared at the floor. It felt as if all my energy, my focus, were ebbing away. As if life itself were departing my body, leaving only emptiness.

"That was back in the peach time. Had peaches on our property. Used to pick 'em with my uncle. Paid me by the basket. Worked all day sometimes, got so I couldn't stand no peaches. The grass was long there, and green. And…"

Tears had begun trickling down my face, I realized. I made no move to wipe them away.

"And we used to play, Bucky and me. He had a ball, like a rubber ball, he liked. Used to throw it for him, have him fetch it through the peach trees. Dog loved that ball. He…"

I was sobbing now, uncontrollably. I hadn't cried since I was a child yet now the tears came, a flood of them, pouring from my eyes and over my face and running down my neck. My throat was thick, sour. I could hardly breathe.

"Oh, ma'am," he said, suddenly realizing. He stood, went to his sink, ran some water into a glass. He set it on the table beside me. "Ma'am, don't do that. Don't cry. Ain't no reason to cry 'bout nothin'."

But I didn't stop. Not for a long time. I drank the lukewarm, bitter water. He stood near me nervously, obviously a stranger to him, a stranger who'd accused him of horrible things and who'd undergone an emotional collapse in front of him for reasons he didn't understand, for reasons he couldn't even imagine.

"I appreciate," he said quietly, "your takin' me to the store. I surely do."

I nodded finally, wiping my eyes, standing shakily.

"It was—nothing," I said.

I made my way outside again, into the blinding sun. McCoy stood there in the doorway, hunched over, all but dead.

Stepping into my car, I started the engine. I sat there shivering, tears trickling down my face, staring through the windshield at the nothingness before me.

"'Bye, ma'am," he wheezed. "Good luck to you."

"Goodbye," I whispered, after a moment. But far too quietly for him, or anyone, to hear.

I drove away.

When I got back to Tucson I called my editor in New York, got him to agree to a three-month delay on the newest Flat-Head Fred story, and checked myself into a hospital. There isn't much to be said about it except that when I checked out again forty-five days later, I no longer drank.

The world looked different when I left the hospital. The colors weren't as bright, the sounds not as vivid. And yet everything was clearer than it had been in a very long time.

I wondered what I would do with myself now, especially in the evenings, alone in the house. Naturally the first thing I did on returning home was to pour all the remaining alcohol into the kitchen sink. Then I opened every window, sat down, and let the dry Arizona breeze fill my lungs.

Okay, Lucy, I'll come with you, I imagined myself saying. *Let me put on my shoes.*

Loss. So many once here, now gone.

I was in a foster home when I learned what had happened

to Lucy, but by then it was later, the flashing lights had come in the night and the police had taken away my parents while Alba held me in my bedroom and said *Don't look, don't look.* I was in another town, not far from Fresno but an intergalactic distance from it for a child. They were a couple, they had other kids; their faces, their names are blurred now. I was with them for a few months, then I was with others: a succession of others, an army of others. It came on the news one night when I was sitting in the corner of someone's living room, drawing. I'd turned thirteen. No one had told me anything. Neither my aunt nor my uncle had ever called or written. If there were any legal repercussions to my having assisted in the theft of a VW Bus and its subsequent damage, I never heard about it; a steel curtain had slammed down on my life in Quiet, California, and now, eight or nine months later, I hardly remembered it. I hardly remembered my parents. I hardly remembered anything at all. And so when a familiar name from what seemed my distant past, Mike McCoy, was spoken, I looked up. There he was, being led into a courtroom in a prison outfit. I heard the names Maria Sanchez, Trista Blake, Lucy Sparrow. But there were no photos, and the story was over practically before it had begun. I understood that he had murdered those people, but the name *Lucy Sparrow* seemed to have almost no connection with me. She was someone I'd once known long ago, briefly been childhood friends with. The memories were gone, seared away to oblivion.

Where are we going, Lucy?

My life after that a long smear of pain. I never saw my parents again; they were in prison for years, then died in an auto crash shortly after they were released. People flitted in and out of my life: caregivers, teachers, friends. I learned to smile a lot, show my dimples. When I smiled people stopped asking what was wrong, stopped saying, *Cheer up, things can't be that bad!* I was an automaton, saying the right things, smiling on cue. I did very well in school, all schools, and there were many: three or four different high schools, in fact. Sometimes I noticed looks of pity being directed at me, usually by female teachers. I despised them. But I smiled.

Let's go to Mike's, I heard her say in my imagination. *I wanna learn how to play pool, Franny-Fran.*

And I drew. Drew and wrote stories. Eventually I was in college, where I also did well. Flat-Head Fred and Mary the Motor Scooter date from those years: they were two among dozens of characters I created then, in rough prototype form. To escape my childhood memories I ended up creating works that would generate memories for other children. Perhaps there's some good in it.

No, Lucy, I don't want to go there. Let's just stay under the pepper tree together. In the dark. And in the morning they'll wonder where we are and we'll just be here, right here, safe and sound.

The faces, the voices: thirty years gone. Have I remembered it correctly? Was this really the way it was?

Okay, let's do it. We'll just stay here. I won't go to Mike's at all.

Lucy, have I written it right?

Let me brush your hair, Lucy. I'll brush it all night.

…Or am I still a spaz?

We'll just stay here 'til the sun comes up. Then we'll see what'll happen tomorrow. There's always tomorrow.

Lucy, I tried to save you. When you came to my window, we could have stayed together; we could have done anything we wanted to do. We still had that night, that one final night. There wasn't any tomorrow. None at all. Lucy. Lucy.

I knocked softly on my daughter's bedroom door.

For a moment there was no response.

She knew I was coming; I'd talked to Donald about it, about the possibility of my stopping by their house, seeing her for just a few minutes. Alone.

I don't have any right to ask, Donald. But…

I'll see, Frances. I'll ask Jess what she thinks about it.

"Come in."

I opened the door. She was on her bed, facing away from me, head propped up on her elbow. She was thumbing through a book. She wore her usual T-shirt and jeans; her feet were covered with pink socks with little fuzzy balls on their ends. For once her baseball cap wasn't on her head; her hair was down, loose over her shoulders. I could see her face only in profile as she stared down at the book.

I stepped in, closed the door softly behind me.

"Jess," I said quietly, "is it okay with you that I'm here?"

She shrugged.

I looked around her room. It was the room of an athletic twelve-year-old girl. Her softball uniform was sprawled on the floor; there was a soccer ball in the corner. Posters of sports stars competed with posters of young TV hunks for wall space.

"How are you, Jess?"

She shrugged again.

I looked at her. Though she was a sturdy, athletic girl, she suddenly seemed hopelessly fragile to me, as if she might shatter completely in the first gust of wind that came her way. I wanted to wrap my arms around her, protect her forever, save her. And yet I was the person from whom she'd needed to be saved.

I sat down gingerly behind her on the corner of the bed.

"What are you reading?" I asked.

She held it up over her shoulder: it was *Mary's Amazing*

Morning, one of the early Mary the Motor Scooter books.

"Oh my gosh, Jess. That one goes back to when you were little."

"I know," she said. "I remember you drawing it."

"Do you really?" I was surprised; she must have been very young.

"Sure. I used to watch you. I was, like, in awe of you. That you could draw like that. And write those stories."

I leaned over, looking at the page she had open. It was an illustration of a happy-looking Mary making a milkshake. As I stared at the drawing it occurred to me for the first time that Mary not only looked like Jess—that had been deliberate—but also a bit like Lucy Sparrow. The same eyes, the wild dirty-blonde hair. I'd never noticed before.

"I like this one," she said. "It's my favorite."

"I didn't know you had favorites," I said. "Of those books, I mean."

"Sure I do. I still read them sometimes."

"Not the newer ones, I'm sure."

"Yeah, I do." She pointed to her bookcase across the room where, indeed, there was a long line of Mary and Fred books. I always gave her a copy of each one, of course. But I didn't imagine she read them. I thought perhaps she threw them away. "I like the earlier ones better. The later ones are…I don't know. Kind of sad, sometimes."

"I guess they are."

There was a long silence. She turned the pages.

"Dad says that you've been working really hard."

"Working…?"

"At that place. That clinic."

"Well—yes."

"But you're done with it now."

"Done? Well, honey, I—I hope so. I hope I'm done. I'm

going to try to be done. I'm going to try as hard as I can."

"That's cool," she said, looking at Mary the Motor Scooter. "Lots of cool people go to rehab. Like, famous people."

I didn't know what to say. I was about to stand up and go—I didn't want to overstay my welcome. But, without consciously intending it, I found myself lying down behind her on the bed. I touched her waist gently.

"Is it okay?" I asked. "Just for a minute?"

Another shrug. "You're my mom."

But after a while she closed the book and her head dropped to her pillow. I felt her body relax, ease slowly into mine.

We didn't say anything.

I breathed the scent of her hair. I knew that I was on my last chance with my daughter, my absolutely final chance—that if I failed this time I'd be cast out from her life forever. Therefore I couldn't fail. The ouroboros had to unwind at last, open the endless circle that had been closed for so long.

After a time, unable to stop myself, I whispered, "Jess, I love you."

And later—very, very much later, so much later that I thought I might never hear her voice again in this life—I heard her whisper to me in return, nearly inaudibly, but audibly: "I love you too."

In my dream Lucy Sparrow stands facing me in the night surf, fists on her hips, waves bursting softly about her thighs, looking much as I remember her at twelve when the two of us were best friends forever: blood sisters. She wears no bathing suit, but isn't exactly naked; instead her body appears featureless, like a doll's, lacking nipples or navel, freckles or scars—incomplete, unfinished. Yet her face is as it was in life. The big raincloud-colored eyes, the shapeless nose, the tangled dirty-blonde hair splayed to her shoulders.

Little happens in the dream. She just stares at me, her expression flat, unreadable—neither friendly nor hostile—while from the shore I whisper over and over, a hot ache pulsing in my throat: *Lucy. Lucy.* There's a sudden shriek overhead (a bird? a bat?) but this time I know not to look away. After a moment Lucy begins to walk toward me, stops when she reaches the surf's edge. She beckons to me.

I step to her, noticing that I'm not the little girl that I was then. I've grown up. I know that I'm middle-aged, a writer of children's books, a mother, an alcoholic. But my appearance seems not to affect her. She drops to her knees and begins digging in the wet sand. I kneel to help her.

After a while we bring up a sand-encrusted Mason jar. Lucy runs it through the surf once to clean it off. We look at it together, smiling. Our time capsule. Never finished, in life. Finished here.

She strips away the tape we used thirty years before to seal it and unscrews the lid. It comes away easily. She reaches inside and together we look at what we put there so long ago. School photos of each of us, perfectly preserved. A map of the town as it was then, so different from now. Newspaper headlines with names like Ford and Kissinger and Rockefeller. Clippings from magazines—one picture of Donny Osmond, half a dozen of John Travolta.

Finally she pulls out our drawings. There's mine, the illustration of the two of us floating together with angels' wings, but it's completed now, luminously colored-in. Behind us in the picture float dozens, even hundreds of angels departing the earth, as if this were the jumping-off point for every angel in the world, a matrix of angels stepping off into an endless sky. My neat, precise inscription is at the bottom: *For Lucy, With All My Love, Franny-Fran.*

Finally Lucy brings forth the last item in the jar. It's her own drawing. She moves to hand it to me, but the wind catches it; the paper swoops and dives and lands finally in the surf. I leap to grab it before the picture on the sheet is obliterated forever, but it's too late. Holding it up in the moonlight, I can make out only a single part of the image she's drawn: a pair of big silver hearts entwined. But the wet ink loosens, slides down the paper; the hearts look for a moment strangely like angels' wings before they drop away, melt irretrievably into the sea. Lucy's heart. Mine.

By the time I look toward her again, I'm alone in the darkness.

Author's Note

Truman Capote once wrote a friend about a work in progress, "I have a novel, something on a large and serious scale, that pursues me like a crazy wind." The phrase encapsulates my experience with *A Matrix of Angels*—I felt that "crazy wind" whipping at me for nearly two years, in a way unlike anything else I've ever written, pushing me to discover the final form of the story of Fran and Lucy.

The novel began life as a long short story, also titled "A Matrix of Angels," which, in a moment of misdirected altruism, I gave to a publisher who was soliciting stories for a charity anthology. Alas, like many such efforts, the book—unreviewed, mostly unread—sank like a stone immediately upon its publication, taking my piece with it. Naturally I was frustrated. But even before this debacle, I'd noticed something odd about this story, this theme, these characters. In every previous instance of my writing life, when a story was finished, I was done with it. However much the plot and people had preoccupied me before and during the writing, they would vanish from my mind like a forgotten dream after it, never to be revisited—so much so that by the time a work was published I would sometimes be startled by its content, which seemed nearly as fresh to me as if the piece had been written by someone else entirely.

Not so with "A Matrix of Angels." In the year or so after I completed the story, I found my imagination swirling back again and again to Fran and Lucy—they seemed to pursue me like that crazy wind. New scenes and dialogue came to my mind, ideas that I initially resisted—the story was *done,* after all—but which I eventually began noting down. Yet the voices of these two girls still didn't stop, and finally I realized I needed to start all over again—not to expand the original story, but to take an entirely fresh approach.

I ultimately completed the novel version of *A Matrix of Angels* over several summer months, never consulting the short story—this was to be an entirely new work, not an adaptation of something already written. When it was finished the voices of Fran and Lucy grew silent at last, and I knew that the tale had finally, truly, reached its end.

While I consider the novel to be the definitive version of this material, it's a pleasure to unearth the original story and present it here. Whatever its flaws, Fran and Lucy first saw the light of day in this much briefer work—a work I'd believed complete in itself, until the crazy wind blew my way.

C.C.

A Matrix of Angels
The Original Short Story

1

THIRTY-SIX DAYS BEFORE Lucy Sparrow was abducted and murdered by the Riverbed Killer (who turned out to be a local dropout we both knew named Mike McCoy, then working at the nearby Red Ball gas station; we both knew him), she and I met for the first time at the school bus stop. This was thirty years ago. More than ten thousand mornings away.

Lucy came rushing out her front door at the last possible moment, just as the big yellow bus—the "cheese bus," the other students called it—was rounding the curve from Thumbelina Avenue and rumbling up Kendale Road. I checked my watch: eight-fourteen, on the nose. I was waiting a full ten minutes beforehand, but Lucy only appeared just as the bus itself was pulling up. Since she had to cross the street, she would have to run in front of the vehicle to reach the door, before it had come to a complete stop. This earned a blaring honk from the driver, Mr. Cox, who cried indignantly, "No running in front of the bus!" as she mounted the steps breathlessly.

All this I would recognize as routine only later. On that first day as the new girl at Soames Middle School in Quiet, California, a few miles inland from the Pacific Ocean, I knew only that I had been told to meet the bus at the corner at exactly eight-fourteen a.m., that if I weren't there Mr. Cox would not wait, that if I failed to appear the bus would leave without me and I would be left to explain why I had been unable to perform such a simple task. And to expect punishment commensurate with such a venal and intolerable crime.

The people with whom I was living, not my parents, were a phlegmatic distant cousin of my father's named Frank and his wife Louise. By issuing such dire warnings they proved that they did not know their girl. Having been with them only a few weeks, they could have no idea that order, routine, punctuality, *control,* were the hallmarks of my existence. Never for me the unfinished chore, the neglected homework assignment, the missed bus, all of which seemed to me mere invitations to chaos and disaster. Never for me the hair out of place, the stained T-shirt, the dirty or ragged fingernail. Thus—needless to say—in every school I ever attended I was quickly branded as "stuck up," yet it was not a belief in my superiority that made me act this way; it was my absolute conviction that I was hopelessly inferior to everyone else, so much so that all I could do was try to be as close to perfect as I possibly could, in the desperate hope that others might at least learn to tolerate me. To be *accepted* was only a forlorn dream.

So it was eight-fourteen on a gray morning in March—March the eleventh, in fact, as indicated under "Date of Entry" on the Soames Middle School report card I still possess—that I first beheld Lucy Sparrow crashing out her front door, slamming it shut behind her and charging heedlessly into the street. She was wearing sandals, blue jeans, and a tattered T-shirt—which, all these years later, I can state with confidence because in the slightly more than a month that I knew her, I never saw Lucy Sparrow wear anything else. There were different colored shirts, but they were all the same, all of them badly worn and frayed. She would wear the same shirt for a week, having found it on her bedroom floor in the same place she deposited it every night. Only when I would point out that it reeked to high heaven would she lift her arm, stick her nose into her armpit and inhale. "Mmm-yeah!" she would call out. "Lucy's *ripe*!" But she would change the shirt.

She was a tomboy, and not particularly pretty. Her face was square, blockish; her most typical expression was a scowl, and when she smiled an auxiliary chin would appear. She was not fat, but she was heavily built, with muscular arms and breasts preternaturally developed for a sixth-grader. Girls didn't like her because she was loud, rude; boys found her unnerving. And yet later I would see that, when she was in a peaceful, reflective mood, her face relaxed and happy, she would have moments of startling beauty: the hard angles would dissolve, her icy blue eyes soften, and her blonde, nearly silver hair, invariably tangled and rat's-nested, would bounce and glisten. This was a Lucy few would ever see. I myself saw her hardly at all, yet my memory of those few occasions remains as vivid as any memories I have. I found her mesmerizing to look at, a rough, blowsy, hard-edged angel.

That first morning, however, the encounter was limited to my backing away from the bus door as this hurricane of a girl came rushing up to it, backpack slung carelessly over her shoulder. "New?" she said, glancing at me in the moment it took for the door to slide open. I nodded. "Good luck—you'll need it," she said, turning away and mounting the first step. Over her shoulder she added, "This place is a fuckin' dump!"

As homicidal maniacs go, the Riverbed Killer was a small-timer. He claimed only three victims, of whom Lucy Sparrow was the last. His entire spree lasted a mere two weeks, not even long enough for the community to begin to panic—by the time the bodies began to be discovered he was already dead, shot down in a police chase outside Santa Barbara. This was only days after Lucy's body was found, what was found of it, in the dry riverbed off the freeway: strewn about in pieces, like the other two. Compared to the Gacys and Dahmers of the world, the Riverbed Killer's case contains nothing especially memorable. And yet today, on the more comprehensive websites devoted to serial murderers (and I cannot help but wonder what sort of people create these sites), there he is. There are his victims. Trista Sanchez, Tina Blake, and Lucy, who looks much as I remember her, although I've not seen even a photo of her in thirty years. In fact, she looks exactly the same, except that it seems impossible she could have been so young—or that I could. The picture is in black and white, no doubt scanned from an old newspaper story or yearbook. Lucy Sparrow.

And there are pictures of the investigation, as well, old news shots of local police and Santa Barbara County detectives standing in the riverbed, sorting through debris. There are no photos, thank God, of the actual crime scenes. It's strange for me to realize that such photographs must exist today, buried in the ancient, disused files of law enforcement agencies and news organizations in central California. Somewhere, if one only knew where, one could go to an old file cabinet, open it, and draw forth a sheaf of papers which would include images of what was left of Lucy Sparrow when they found her. For that, if anything, turns out to be the Riverbed Killer's sole distinguishing point: the sheer brutality of his methods. The basement he had outfitted with ball-and-chain, lockable metal staples set into concrete walls, a bed with leather restraining devices such as one finds in mental asylums, a Spanish Inquisition-style "rack." And his tools: sledgehammers, knives, sharpened screwdrivers, a band saw, a high-powered electric drill with a huge assortment of drill bits. There was a specially-constructed drain in the middle of the floor. All this he had purchased or built himself. The drill appeared to be his favorite instrument of all. Each victim's skull contained dozens of sharply-defined, cleanly-made holes which investigators somehow knew were drilled—some of them, at least—while the victims were alive. I don't know how anyone can determine such facts. I tell myself I don't believe them. But I do.

At that age, friendships among girls are mercurial, fast-fading; today's best friends for life are tomorrow's bitterest arch-enemies. This is the age when the worst female qualities—and they *are* female qualities: bitchiness, backstabbing, rumor-mongering—come to the fore, with no counterbalancing sense of empathy or pity. If it's true that hell is other people, then surely one division of that hell can be found among the girls of any typical middle school.

Lucy Sparrow was a denizen of such a hell, though I did not see that clearly then. With her smelly clothes, bellowing voice, and boyish ways, she was a perfect target for the girls I quickly identified as the important ones, the "in" crowd: Susie Shaw, Michelle Price, Melissa Deaver, pretty little ego machines who painted their nails at recess and talked about their hair and shoes and argued over who was hotter, Shaun Cassidy or Andy Gibb. I had known such girls at my earlier school, in Stockton, and feared them. I knew my shyness, my virtual terror of human interaction would cause them to create new nick-names for me, as indeed it did: "Miss Stuck-up," of course, but also—within just a few days of my arrival—"Bitchy Britches," and, most memorably, in reference to my physique, "Concentration Camp."

Lucy had it worse. From the very first day, sitting in Mrs. Peterson's homeroom, I heard whisperings.

"Lezzie's here today."

"Yeah, Dyke-o-rama's back."

"Michelle, you really should kiss her. She likes *you* best."

"Eww! *You* kiss her."

Lucy could hardly have failed to hear these remarks—she was only two seats in front of these girls—but her head remained angled over the book she was reading, her hair tumbling over her face so that I could not read her expression. Since I knew she lived across the street from my house, I naturally felt that we might be friends.

We had all our classes together, but Lucy and I did not speak until lunchtime. I had yet to say a word that day other than a few murmured "hellos," and was sitting on the grass looking absently at a group of boys running up and down the field when a loud *thwack* startled me into looking to my right, where the tetherball pole stood. Few seventh-graders used it, I would learn; tetherball was considered kids' stuff, for the elementary schoolers who took their lunch an hour before us. But there was Lucy, slamming away at the ball with her closed fist. She would hit it, watch it with hawklike intensity as it swung around on its rope, and then smash it again, grunting. I watched her for what seemed quite a long time, the ball angling into the air, swooping and dropping, Lucy's fist punching at it. She never missed, and she hit hard. Like a boy, I thought.

"Hi," she said finally, glancing at me, sweat glistening on her forehead. She kept on watching and striking, watching and striking. "Wanna try?"

I swallowed nervously, but managed to stand up and approach her. The ball glided toward my head.

"Go on, hit it, hit it!" she cried.

I swung at it with the heel of my palm, connected rather feebly. It swung lethargically back toward her.

"Look, like this," she said, showing me her clenched fist. "*Wham!*" As she said it, she sent the ball hurling back around in fast circles again, and I found myself ducking away from it.

This made Lucy laugh, the first time I'd heard her do so. It was a big, raucous sound, far larger than one would imagine for someone her size. "Don't be chicken," she said. "C'mon, try!"

I stepped back toward the ball, closed my fist, and swung, missing it completely, which, surprisingly, didn't make her laugh again: in fact, it silenced her. On its next revolution, Lucy grabbed the ball and held it, looking at me.

"Look, c'mere, I'll show you." I hesitated. "*C'mere*," she insisted, and I moved toward her. "Hit it with the side of your fist, like this." She illustrated. "You've gotta keep your eye on the ball. You missed because you looked away. Here, see?" To my surprise, she reached down, grabbed my hand. "Make a fist. Right. Now hit it like this." She pressed the side of my fist against the ball. "Okay? Now, look. Step back. I'll swing it at you, just gentle. See if you can hit it like I showed you." I was afraid she would sock it again, but no, she lofted it softly around the pole so that it arrived, smoothly and slowly, near my raised fist. I swung, connected imperfectly, and the ball spun off in the other direction. "Not bad," she said, catching it. "Here, try again. Now watch it, keep your eye on it."

For the next several minutes I swung my arm at the ball, gradually getting better at it, while she and I talked—or rather, she asked questions and I answered them. How did I like the school? How did I like Mrs. Peterson? Mr. Thorndyke? And what was my name, anyway?

"Fran," I said, preparing to swing. "Fran Carpenter. It's really Frances, but people call me Fran."

"Fran. Hm. Girlie name. Oh, well. I'm Lucy."

And with that we were friends. On some level Lucy frightened me, her aggressiveness and insistence, but on the other hand, she seemed to be taking an interest in me, something no one at my other schools had ever done. I knew that I was spending time with a misfit, that the important girls were probably watching right now, already branding me a loser—hanging around with Lucy Sparrow, playing a little kid's game!—as indeed they were, and did. But it didn't matter. Swatting away at that silly tetherball, I abruptly found myself feeling, for a few moments at least, quite happy.

When the bell rang ending the lunch period, Lucy took the ball for a few final swats. Scowling, she said, "This one's for Susie *Shaw*," slamming the ball as she uttered the last name; it swung around, then she grabbed it again and said, "This one's for Michelle *Price*," and the thing whirled around once more; finally, "This one's for Melissa *Deaver*!" The ball spun crazily around the pole as, giggling wildly, best pals already sharing a secret, we ran off to class.

It turned out that we were both newcomers, aliens to the undistinguished town of Quiet, California. Lucy and her mother had only arrived in November, four months earlier. Their home, as I had seen it from across Kendale Road, was a wreck; cans, trash, and car parts were spread across the yard ("Most of it's the landlord's," Lucy would say, "but we get blamed for it"). The lawn itself, what there was of it, was patchy and brown, dead. As for the house itself, its paint was cracked and chipped everywhere; one front window was held together by strips of masking tape. "My mom rents it," Lucy told me that first afternoon. "She's a waitress." She pointed vaguely. "That's where she is now." What a contrast it was to my aunt and uncle's house, which was much larger and beautifully maintained, with a pristine lawn kept up by a team of weekly maintenance men.

"The neighbors hate us," Lucy would say later. "Mr. Silva called my mom a pig to her face. I was there. But she can't *afford* any better."

She invited me to her house after school that first day, and I felt as nearly salacious thrill at the idea of stepping into such an abode of ill repute, so different from my own home, my own obsessively organized life. "C'mon over," she had said. "I get bored as shit." Aunt Louise had acquiesced when I arrived home, nodding in her dour way, saying only, "Keep out of trouble," before returning her attention to her TV game show and Marlboro cigarettes. (I never quite knew why she watched the shows; she never seemed to take any pleasure in them, never smiling, never laughing. Yet she never missed them, especially *Match Game* and *Family Feud*.)

I found my heart beating fast as I rang Lucy's doorbell.

"Hi," she said, opening the door and grinning. "Welcome to Dumpland!"

A friend, I thought. *My friend!*

Inside the house was a shambles too. Dirty clothes lay everywhere, soiled dishes, old magazines and newspapers; there was an open box of tampons on the kitchen table in the midst of dozens of spilled cigarettes and empty Coors beer cans. A broken chair lay forlornly in the corner, one leg snapped in half. The living room carpet, what there was of it, had once been blue, but it was covered now with brown and yellow and orange stains. To my sense of order there was something shocking about the scene, as if I were looking at someone naked: Dirty people lived here, it seemed to me, *filthy* people. I was obscurely thrilled.

"Who takes care of you when your mom's not home, Lucy?" I asked as we treaded through a dark hallway toward her bedroom.

"Takes care of me? Nobody takes *care* of me," she said. "I take care of myself."

Though I had gone through many difficulties, particularly when my parents forced me to travel to this little town hundreds of miles from where I'd grown up in order to live with Frank and Louise (*Why? What did I do? What did I do?*), I had never, then or now, come home to an empty house: first my mother, then Louise had always been there, with the sound of the TV or their voices on the telephone—something, at least, to ensure that I wasn't coming home to loneliness, silence, death. *There's no one home,* I thought to myself in horror, studying Lucy. *There's no one home here, no one at all.*

"We can go to my house, Lucy," I said. "My aunt's there."

She scowled. "Why? That's a stupid idea."

Her bedroom was exactly like the rest of the house. Her clothes covered the floor to such a complete degree that the carpet couldn't be seen at all; her bed was unmade; there were stuffed animals in tumbledown confusion on every shelf and window sill. A few magazines were scattered on the floor, some of them open and gaping. There was an old record player in one corner and collapsing heaps of 45s next to it. Such a contrast to my own room, the bed made to nearly military standards of perfection, clothes washed, ironed, and hung in the closet, bookshelf with its titles alphabetized and well-dusted, schoolbooks stacked by size on the desk, pencils sharpened to a fine point and waiting in a jar. And still, I knew, still I was not good enough.

"Let's play some tunes," Lucy said, putting a 45 on the record player: Boston's "More Than a Feeling." I watched her from the doorway as she danced lightly with the music, eyes closed, tousling her hair. "My mom gets these records from the jukebox at work," she told me. "Once people don't play them anymore, the owner gets rid of them and gets new ones. I mean, he just throws them *away.* So I get them now. It's cool. The only thing is, they're kind of old. But some of them are great. I listen to them all the time. Music just *does* something to me."

I sat down gingerly on the bed. The sheets, I noticed, smelled. I took a stuffed tiger in my hands and looked at it.

"That's Gus-Gus," she said, smiling as she danced. "All of these guys have names, every one. There's Gilbert and Short Stack and Miss Mooch, Boo-Boo and Rag Bag and Big Sam…I guess I have like fifty or sixty. And I love 'em *all*."

I was surprised—I certainly hadn't associated Lucy Sparrow with anything like cute stuffed animals. I suspected Melissa Deaver and her ilk hadn't either. I felt that I was being allowed to peer into Lucy's secret heart, to see aspects of her that no one else saw. It was a strange, exhilarating feeling.

I should explain that, for whatever reason, I did not then (nor do I now) possess a gift for friendship. I was always the child who sat in the corner studying her book, never participating in games or sports unless I was forced to. When that happened, I invariably embarrassed myself, falling and skinning my knee at hopscotch, striking out or dropping the ball in softball. I was humiliated by my body, my buck teeth, my skinny frame that caused other children to call me "Skeleton" or "Scarecrow." I was smart, I knew, but I also knew that I would trade all the brains in my head for the kind of personality and grace that would allow me to be part of the lives of the other kids, the ones who mattered.

So what for anyone else would have been just a minor, quickly forgettable hour or two at a friend's house was, for me, something quite extraordinary. In fact, I was not only amazed at Lucy; I was amazed at myself. Whatever shallow pools of self-confidence I had ever possessed when I lived with my parents were utterly depleted that strange morning I was made to board a bus to Santa Barbara, of all places, for "a little visit with your aunt and uncle"—even though I knew, bewildered as I was, that for *a little visit* I couldn't possibly need as much luggage as was being sent along with me. *Why do I have to go? Are you coming too?* For all our apparent wealth—modest, but wealth—I was dimly aware that not all girls lived with parents who used needles and syringes in the middle of the night, who seemed to pass out for days on end, who had peculiar people visiting the house at odd hours; parents who would constantly warn (in a gentle, humorous tone, yet with cold steel in it) *Don't tell anyone what goes on here.* I knew, I knew! I was a bright girl, I didn't have to be taught twice. I learned my lessons and lived by them. Of course I told no one. I kept my body, my clothes, all my possessions as neat as humanly possible, as perfect as they could be, so that I myself might become worthy of the two of them, worthy of anyone, that someone—Mom or Dad or some bright stranger—would come to me at last and say: *You've done wonderfully, you're an angel on earth, I love you, little girl, I love you.*

Instead there had been the bus one gray Saturday morning, the suitcases, the claims that I would remember Uncle Frank and Aunt Louise as soon as I saw them, the assurances that it's just for a little while, honey, your dad and I have to work some things out, we'll see you soon, *Mom it's the middle of the school year, why, what's happening?* Hush, Franny, just hush, have a lovely trip, you'll hear from us soon.

I was too stunned even to cry, sitting breathless and wide-eyed on the bus seat for hours, adrift, my moorings gone. Nothing changed when I arrived at the bus station and was greeted by a gray-haired man and woman who, I was quite certain, I had *not* met before, and driven for what seemed a long time to this small house in the middle of a housing track in this dusty, nondescript town. *When do I get to be with my parents again?* Soon, soon.

From then on I hardly spoke, hardly made eye contact with anyone, which made my visit with Lucy Sparrow all the more remarkable. Some part of me knew that I should not risk friendship, not place in jeopardy my safe and orderly self, yet Lucy was so open and giving that I could hardly help looking at her with gratitude and love from that first day, this girl who was loud and smelly and obviously poor, this girl who put the Wings record "My Love" on her little player and said, "C'mon, slow dance with me, I'll pretend you're a boy," and, astonishingly, I did, I stood and allowed her to place her heavy arms around me, allowed her to lead me in slow circles in her bedroom until I finally raised my arms to her shoulders as well. Holding on. Holding on for dear life.

2

FROM THEN WE were inseparable. We sat together on the bus, played tetherball and soccer at recess—not real games, just the two of us kicking the ball back and forth, laughing, tumbling hysterically into the grass—and passed notes to each other in Math and Science and English. (What did we write so feverishly about? I can't imagine, now.) I would stay for hours with her at her house, doing homework—or really, helping her, since Lucy was a weak student. I would be shocked to see an essay she'd written or some Math problems she'd attempted to solve; she was far behind me in ability, despite the fact that she was actually a year older than me, at thirteen officially a *teenager* ("I was held back one year"). Occasionally, or perhaps more than that, I simply did her work for her, though she never asked me for this service. Partly I was angry—not with her, but with the adults in her life who, I perceived, had been so criminally negligent with her education, with *her*. But mostly I just wanted to please her, to make her happy, this girl who had chosen me among all the dozens of others she might have chosen, the one and only person who had looked at me and thought, *Yes, I find you acceptable, I want you to be my friend.*

"C'mon, Franny-Fran," she would say. "I can write the stupid essay myself. Though I'll admit I like the grades you get for me. Except they're never A's!"

"Mrs. Mainer wouldn't believe it if you turned in an A essay, Lucy," I said, honestly. "She'd think you copied it."

She nodded. "You're right. I'm not good with essays, am I? Shit, I'm not good with school."

"It's not your fault. Here, let me show you." And we would pour over the assignment together, with me attempting to encourage Lucy's participation while still ensuring that the final product would arrive safely in the B range—such a change from her usual D's and F's.

Lucy sometimes visited my house (though I didn't think of it that way; I thought of it as Frank and Louise's house), but not as often. It was clear that, for whatever reason, Louise did not like Lucy. She would merely grunt a greeting when we came in, frowning and muttering some instruction to *keep it down* or *not make a mess*. As a result, we would stay mostly at Lucy's. Her mother was almost never there, and this fact, which had once seemed so shocking, began to be attractive. We turned on records as loud as we wanted, dancing and singing along to them. We ate whatever we found in the refrigerator. We played Nerf football in the living room, knocking over vases and pictures. I read stories to her from my favorite books, fantasy tales about unicorns and fairies and angels. We watched TV together, but not much: TV was dulling to the mind, soporific, and what I wanted, needed—we both did— was just the opposite. Instead, Lucy would turn on her radio at seven p.m. and tune in a station from Los Angeles, a fading, wavery but listenable signal, and we would sit together, often in the dark, as the news headlines drifted by and then the creaking door of the *CBS Radio Mystery Theater* opened. "I love this show," she would say. "With TV you see things, but with radio you see *clear.*" We would burrow together under our blanket, hand in hand, munching popcorn or candy, listening raptly. Sometimes I would brush her hair as we listened, carefully untangling it in dozens of places, smoothing it with my palm. The stories—mystery, science fiction, surprisingly grisly horror—sometimes made us squeal with fright, or what we pretended to each other was fright.

Soon enough—too soon, always too soon!—eight o'clock would arrive, and with it my curfew, my forced return to the exile that was supposed to be my home. In bed I would feel an aching loneliness, an actual physical sensation in the pit of my stomach. Lucy was so close then, only across the street, but as far away as if she'd lived in another galaxy.

Naturally the popular girls in school looked askance at our friendship. It made no difference to us. Suddenly the taunts that had been so hurtful before seemed only silly, childish. There was never any threat of physical violence—Lucy was by far the biggest and strongest girl in the school, no one would have imagined trying to fight her—and so it never went farther than the occasional muttered "Lezzies" or "Dykes" as we passed by in the hall. We found it fantastically funny. (At her house we would play-act as these girls, pretending to be them and creating riotous send-ups of their personalities and mannerisms.) Once as we wandered along the edge of the football field we heard several girls chanting, "*Lu*cy and *Fran*ny sittin' in a *tree*, *k-i-s-s-i-n-g!*" Lucy stopped, glanced back at them, and then grabbed my head and kissed me straight on the lips. It was as un-erotic as a kiss could possibly be, and we dissolved into shrieks of laughter. Those girls never chanted anything at us again.

I would like to report that we had many deep, soul-sharing conversations, but in truth we did not, at least until the end. I did not ask, did not *think* to ask, what had become of Lucy's father; and I have no recollection of ever telling her about my parents. Instead we had *fun*. In many ways Lucy and I acted younger than we were, silly-girlish, as if together we were discovering the joys of childhood which neither of us had previously known. At that age it's the friendless who suffer; friendship makes one invincible. For the first time in my life, I found myself strong, confident, untouchable. It made no difference if I rounded a corner to hear, "Hey, it's Concentration Camp" or "Here comes Bitchy Britches." I began to think of them as children, as mere naughty kids. I was something else now, something better, something *more*. I even began getting into trouble at school, like other kids did; very mild trouble, it's true, but still, tiny flaws appeared in my armor of perfection. Several times teachers would demand to see the notes Lucy and I had been passing; one even made us change our seats so that we were far apart in his classroom. It made no difference. It was all grist for our imaginations later, our sense of mockery and fun, our feeling that the two of us were a single unassailable unit, and would be forever.

Lucy had an old red Schwinn bicycle, a "boy's bike," as they were still known in those not yet entirely enlightened times. Rusted and dented, it was still serviceable, and we would ride together around the neighborhood in the afternoons or at twilight. I sat behind her, pressed up against her body, my chin on her shoulder, arms wrapped around her waist. Once, I remember, she let me in on what she claimed was a secret: "See that old van there?" she said, stopping the bike for a moment.

"Yes. It's Mr. Silva's."

She glanced mischievously at me. "I drive it sometimes."

"Oh, come on, Lucy, no you don't."

"I swear to God. He leaves his keys in it every night."

"How do you know how to drive?"

"I don't. Not really. But my mom showed me how to shift gears once in her car."

"Where do you go with it?" I asked, deeply skeptical.

She shook her head. "Just around the neighborhood. Late at night I sneak out, just drive it around really slow. I always park it right where it was before."

I dismissed this as Lucy's fantasy, and while I said nothing, I felt slightly disappointed with her, that she would feel the need to lie to me, to *me.* But it was easy enough to let it go, to just enjoy her, to enjoy myself, life.

On Saturdays we would glide into town, sometimes stopping at the grocery store for an ice cream bar or a big sixteen-ounce bottle of Coke we would share and then immediately return for the deposit. There was little in the town, really, to interest two girls like us: no movie theater, no drug store, no fast food restaurants. So we amused ourselves with the comic books in the grocery store, stocked anew each Thursday afternoon by the owner, a large friendly woman named Estelle (she never minded our loitering, our reading without buying: I suspect she knew Lucy was poor, and anyway, we always bought a snack). We wandered around the few shops, rode by the restaurant where Lucy's mother worked—and sometimes went in, managing to cadge free appetizers from her. We went to the library, a lovely old Victorian building, and chatted with the librarian, the unbelievably ancient Mrs. Klibo (she was probably sixty); I would get a book, generally a small paperback which I could stuff into the waistline of my pants for the return ride home, while Lucy flipped through big

Life and *Look* picture books. "You're such a wonderful reader, Fran," Mrs. Klibo would say to me confidentially, out of Lucy's hearing. "I hope you can make your poor little friend a reader too. You'll try, won't you?"

We would laze out in the grass of the tiny park, really a rest stop for travelers from the nearby freeway, sometimes tossing a ball between us or climbing the old oak tree which provided the only available shade. We would hang out for a few minutes at the Red Ball gas station, watching the cars pull in and out and talking with Mr. McCoy, the greasy-looking young man working there in the afternoons who would always invite us to his house. "Got hot dogs and soda," he would say, squinting as he looked at us, grinning, scratching his stomach. "Got games in the basement, too. You girls like ping-pong? How about pool, you like to shoot pool?"

"Ping-pong's okay," Lucy would say casually, chewing on the licorice sticks he always gave us for free from the station's tiny selection of candy. "Never played pool."

"Oughta try. Bet you'd be good at it, big girl like you."

"Maybe sometime, Mr. McCoy."

We would jump on her bike, pedal away.

"I like him," Lucy would say. "He's nice. Kinda weird, though. Looks at me funny."

"Me too," I said.

Naturally Mrs. Sparrow liked me. I was a "good influence," she said. But Aunt Louise, chain-smoking Marlboros and drinking whiskey at three in the afternoon as she watched her game shows, showed nothing but disdain for Lucy. "The Sparrows are trash," she told me one day after school, staring at the TV screen: *Match Game,* Gene Rayburn laughing at some witticism just uttered by Richard Dawson. "Fran, those people are goddamn hicks, just off the tomato truck. Look at all the garbage in their yard. Look at the jalopy that woman drives. I wish we could get them out of the neighborhood somehow. Do they even have indoor plumbing?"

"Yes," I said, looking down, aware of her biting sarcasm but unable to think of any other response. "It's not their house. They rent it."

"I'll bet." She took a drag on her latest cigarette. "You know, Fran, people judge people by the company they keep. I want you to stop hanging around with that Sparrow girl so much. People'll start to think we're the same as them."

"I like her, Aunt Louise. She's my friend."

"There's all kinds of girls to be your friend at that school."

"Not like Lucy."

"Crap. Big butch tomboy, that's all she is. And I got a call from your teacher, Mrs.—what's her name? Stansfield?"

"Stensland."

"Stensland, yeah. She says you're passing notes in class with that girl."

"It was just one note, Aunt Louise," I said, lying.

"Well, cut it out. I don't like the way you're changing, Fran. Ever since you've been friends with that Sparrow girl…"

"It's not Lucy's fault. Don't blame her."

"…you've been staying out late, your grades are dropping…"

"I'm only across the *street,* Aunt Louise. And it was just *one* test I did bad on."

"…and now this, with the notes. I want you to stop hanging around her. No more visits after school. You come straight home."

"That's not fair."

"And stay away from her at school, if you know what's

222 ~ Christopher Conlon

good for you. Don't let somebody like that *drag you down*, Fran."

"She's not dragging me down! You don't understand!"

"Come straight home after school from now on."

"That's *not fair*." Breath heavy, pulse pounding behind my eyes. "Who are you, anyway? You're not my mother!"

Running to my room, slamming the door, collapsing onto the bed. Weeping: my life, I was sure, all but over.

Thus it was that I became a rebel.

A mild-mannered rebel, to be sure; a quiet rebel. But a rebel all the same. For the first time in my life I realized that I did not necessarily have to follow every edict that came down from these anonymous mother- and father-surrogates; I even questioned the authority of my own parents. Who had they been, to send me here? Was it really my fault? Or—and this was an astonishing, a revolutionary thought—was it theirs? Was there, in fact, nothing wrong with me at all? Was it *them*?

I took less care with my appearance, let my room grow sloppy—at least, sloppy by my own standards; it remained rather tidy in comparison with Lucy's. I began to let some homework assignments slide, not enough to get me in any real trouble, but enough to let the teacher and Aunt Louise and the world know that I would no longer blindly kowtow to their every whim—that I was myself, a *person*. In any event, the anti-Lucy edict had relatively little practical effect. We were still together in school all day, and on Saturday morning it was easy enough to tell my aunt and uncle, absolutely honestly, that I was going to the library—and then meet Lucy there. I knew they would never bother to check up on me; they rarely went anywhere but the local bar, from which Lucy and I would keep our distance. We even went to her house at times, when her mother wasn't home, simply by coming around the back way, out of the view of our house, climbing the rear fence and coming in through their back door. The seven p.m. *Radio Mystery Theater* was never more delicious than in those fugitive days, the two of us hunkered under a blanket, giggling, an unstoppable force aligned against a world that was aligned against us.

And then it ended.

I woke to a knocking on my bedroom window. Though it had never happened before, I felt no fear at all: I instantly knew it had to be Lucy, as indeed it was. I pulled open the curtain and lifted the window, the screen dividing us. I glanced at my clock: just past two in the morning. Lucy was crying, something I had never seen her do.

"We're moving," she said, without preamble. "My mom and me."

I looked at her, a horrified sinking sensation in my heart. For a long time I just looked at her, at the tears glistening on her face.

"I'll come out," I whispered.

I slipped on jeans and a T-shirt—in fact it was one of Lucy's, we had quietly traded a few—and crept quietly out in my bare feet. My aunt and uncle were long asleep. The night was warm, nearly humid, with dark clouds obliterating all but a few stars overhead. I had never seen her like this, had always felt that she was *my* rock, *my* support, and yet as we stood there in the darkness I felt stronger than I ever had. I felt important. I felt loved. After all, she had come to *me*.

"Why?" I whispered. "Shh, Lucy, why? Why are you moving?"

"My goddamn fucking dad," she said, her voice shaking wildly.

"What? Lucy, where is your dad? You've never told me."

"I'm supposed to be with him," she said, looking out at the darkness. "That's what the court said when they got the divorce. But my mom took me. We ran off together."

"Why?"

"Because he's a pervert, that's why."

I was twelve; I knew nothing of such things. "What? What's that?"

"A pervert. He—touches me."

"What do you mean, touches you?"

She flashed angry eyes. "In my privates, stupid."

"He…? Why would he do that?"

"Oh, my God!" She turned away. I knew that in some manner I could not fathom I was failing her. "The court didn't believe me. We've been running from him ever since. We make it a year here, six months there. Nothing ever lasts. My mom somehow gets wind that he's catching up and then we run again. She's talking about us going to Mexico."

I was utterly unmoored. "I don't get it. Why does he touch you?"

"Jesus Christ!" She ran off around the side of the house, toward the street. I followed quickly, my feet tingling with the feel of the spiky grass.

She looked back at me, her eyes hurt, bewildered; and finally it clicked, fell into place in my mind. I understood what she meant, saw shadowy men in my mind looming over young girls, their fingers stroking, probing. I had heard of such things, but only vaguely, impersonally.

"Lucy, I'm sorry…I'm sorry I'm such an idiot. I get it now. What you mean. It's dirty."

"Yeah, well." She inhaled, bringing herself under some

control. "I don't want to go to Mexico," she said quietly, intensely. "I don't want to run anymore. I want to be on my own. Fuck Mom *and* Dad. Just go…somewhere."

"All by yourself?" I said, loss draining my voice to a murmur.

She looked out into the night, at nothing. "You could come."

And instantly my heart rushed and flowed with joy. "I want to come, Lucy. I want to. I will. I'll come."

We looked at each other in the darkness.

"C'mon," she said finally.

We rushed up the street. I thought we were running away, simply running, but no: I suddenly realized we were heading straight for Mr. Silva's van. I thought of protesting, but no: I'd put my life in her hands, there was no turning back.

"Can you really drive it?" I asked.

"Shut up and get in."

The doors were unlocked. It was an ancient, decrepit vehicle, perhaps fifteen or twenty years old. Cheap wood paneling was stuck up all over its interior; there were some tools in the back, a few homemade shelves, some blankets, a case of Coca-Cola and a box of crackers. And the key was in the ignition.

"Where are we going?" I asked.

"Away," she answered.

She turned the key and the engine fired into shockingly noisy life. I was certain every light in every house would suddenly come on, that every neighbor would rush out onto their front lawns crying *Thieves! Thieves!* But nothing happened. Lucy pulled on the gearshift and we began to move forward, jerking lightly. My heart was smashing almost through my chest; I was shaking all over. *We're criminals, we're criminals, I'm a criminal,* I kept thinking, a low moan escaping my throat, too soft for Lucy to hear over the engine. And yet for all my terror there was nowhere on earth I would rather have been.

After we were some distance from Mr. Silva's house she switched on the headlights and maneuvered the vehicle with surprising smoothness through two stop signs and we rumbled very slowly into the town, which was entirely dark but for a few streetlamps. Absolutely nothing was open; there was no sign of a single human being anywhere. It was as if we were broken off from the world, gliding along on some distant uninhabited planet, empty yet with all the signs of habitation: buildings, roads. At each moment I believed a police car would suddenly pull in front of us, lights flashing, sirens screaming, and men in blue uniforms would jump out with their guns drawn, firing at the windshield. But, again, nothing happened. We passed the grocery store, the library, the bar at which my aunt and uncle drank, the Red Ball gas station. I had never seen any of this at two in the morning, never seen how ghostly the world is at that hour, how forlorn, how hopeless.

Lucy scowled with concentration as she headed toward the freeway onramp.

I did not protest. Part of me was desperate to cry out, *Lucy, no, let me out, we'll be killed!* But I was silent. I would not let her down. I was with her, would always be with her, now and forever. That was what a friend did. A friend stayed. A friend stayed and listened and didn't send you away, didn't suddenly decide you weren't good enough, didn't touch you where you weren't supposed to be touched, didn't make you feel worthless and dirty. A friend loved you, loved you all the way, never stopped loving you.

We slid onto the onramp and Lucy started to merge onto the freeway. Traffic was sparse, but the fact that there were any cars at all made me hold my breath, clench my eyes shut, keep my fists balled tight against my cheeks. I was going to die, I knew, but I would die with Lucy and so it was all right.

We did not move fast. In fact, we were nowhere near freeway speed, and cars rushed past us on our left. The van's engine sounded labored.

"Is there something wrong with the van?" I managed to ask.

"No, um…Actually I've never shifted it past second gear. Well, here goes nothing." She tried, the gears grinding with a nasty sound. "Shit! *Shit!*" She tried again, but the result was the same. "Goddamn it! Where the fuck is third?"

But despite repeated attempts she never found it, and as a result we moved along at twenty-five or thirty miles an hour. Cars passed us, their headlights playing through the van's interior, passing across our faces. One car honked at us. As the lights from another passed over us I looked at Lucy and realized that she was as scared as I was. And yet as time passed and there were no accidents, no police chases, I felt a strange calm come over me. It was all right. We were all right.

We were heading south, toward the ocean, and soon I could see it on the horizon, black and glittering. "Maybe we better stop," Lucy said. "We could stop, figure out what we want to do. I can't just keep driving like this. *Fuck.*" The van began to swerve in the lane, crossing the white line, and a car just passing us blared its horn. Lucy yanked the wheel. "We have to stop," she said. "Oh, goddamn it, Fran, we have to stop."

"It's okay," I said, calmly confident. "It's okay to stop, Lucy. We'll stop, that's all. Can you pull it in here?"

She tried, but she took the tight turn at the exit too fast and the van scraped against the guardrail, veered back and forth in the lane, felt as if it was going to tip over. And yet I felt calm: I was where I should be, where I was supposed to be.

Finally she brought it under control and pulled jerkily

into the empty parking lot. She put on the brake to stop, but I saw immediately we were directly under a streetlamp. I knew I was thinking more clearly than she was.

"No," I said. "Lucy, pull it over there, where it's dark. In fact, pull it past the parking lot. Can you drive it to the bushes at the end?"

Wordlessly she obeyed, and when we stopped the vehicle was hidden in darkness and obscured by brush. We were safe.

Lucy jumped from the van and ran partway onto the beach. She was making a strange, high-pitched wailing sound, almost like a howl, clutching herself tightly. The ocean's roar filled my ears.

"I'm sorry," she said, but not to me: to the sky, to the water. "I'm sorry, I'm sorry, I'm sorry for…for…whatever I did, whatever…I don't know what I did…Oh my God…"

She dropped onto her knees.

"I'm sorry," she whispered again.

I sat carefully next to her, saying nothing, somehow knowing that there was nothing to say. I knew I just had to be there, to not leave her, to stay with her no matter what.

After a time she seemed to calm. I looked around. The scene was otherworldly, spooky, surreal. Dark shapes surrounded us—sand dunes, I knew, darkness upon deeper darkness, but in the night they could be almost anything: giants, monsters. The waves moved relentlessly forward, relentlessly back.

She stood finally. "I wanna go swimming."

"The water'll be cold."

"I don't care."

She began to strip off her clothes. I had never seen her naked. Her nipples were large, like a grown-up woman's, and she had a shock of pubic hair between her legs. I nearly began to cry: She was so beautiful, the most beautiful thing I had ever seen.

"C'mon," she said. "Do you want to?"

I stood and pulled off my shirt, embarrassed despite everything at my flat child's chest, then my pants, exposing my scrawny, bare child's body. This was something I would never have dreamed of doing in front of anyone but Lucy. She did not laugh at me, call me Scarecrow or Concentration Camp. In fact, she studied me for a moment, then said, "You're pretty, Fran," something no one had ever said to me before, something no one would say again for years. "Don't forget that." Then she turned to the sea.

I followed her joyously. The water was liquid ice, salty and breathtaking. She swam powerfully into the waves, farther and farther, easily outdistancing me, until she was a distant white speck bobbing up and down, until I could hardly see her, until I felt I was alone, set adrift in the universe, naked and lost.

"Lucy?" I whispered. "Lucy? Come back. Please come back. Don't leave me. Don't leave me all alone."

Darkness, the waves crashing, the salt cold, and no voice, no living thing anywhere in the world.

"Lucy," I whispered again. "Please. Lucy."

I shut my eyes, resolved to sink into the waves, vanish into the deep, disappear.

Then, after a while, beside me, came her voice.

"Hi, Franny-Fran."

I turned. She was there, her hair plastered to her head and shoulders, skin glistening palely in the night, and I was all right again, we were all right.

"I thought you'd left me alone," I said.

"I almost did," she admitted. "But— nah."

"I'm glad you came back."

"So am I. But can I tell you a secret?"

"What, Lucy?"

She grinned. "I'm cold as shit!"

I giggled. "So am I!"

We made our way back to the beach and discovered to our horror that we'd left our clothes too near the sea: everything was soaked.

"Never mind," Lucy said, "let's just get back into the car!"

Sodden things bundled in our arms, we rushed back to the van. We brushed off the sand sticking to us and huddled together under the blankets, shivering for a while, warming slowly. This time there was no *Mystery Theater* to hear, only the sounds of our own breathing and the ocean beyond. We calmed, we relaxed. We ate stale crackers, drank warm Coke; they were delicious. I had no brush, but I touched her wet hair tenderly, pulling gently at the tangles, separating the strands, smoothing them with my palm. We said nothing to each other, nothing at all.

After a while it began to rain. My consciousness drifting, I saw visions of unicorns, of fairies and angels in a weightless blue paradise, saw dimly that Lucy was there, floating, an angel herself, I was too, we were both angels in a world of angels, a skyscape of them, a matrix of angels, all of them ourselves and no one else. We fell asleep together, as warm and safe as either of us had ever been, or ever would be again.

We had both dressed and were out in the bushes peeing the next morning when we saw a police car pull up near the van. We looked at each other, and it crossed my mind that we might run, made one final dash over the sand dunes or straight into the sea. But it was over, we knew. Finished.

3

LUCY AND I sat together for the last time on a cold bench in the local police station. Her mother and my aunt were in the office there, talking to someone, there were raised words; but I could make out what they were. I was too shocked, too horrified to cry. Instead I shivered, shivered violently, holding my arms as tightly to myself as I could. I wanted Lucy to tell me that it would be okay, to make a joke, to pretend to be the arresting cop (*You got a license to drive this thing, young lady?*), anything. But she was silent, unblinking, unmoving. My aunt came out first, grabbing my hand and pulling me up off the bench. I had a wild impulse to pull free, to press myself into Lucy's arms, to say *I love you! I love you!* to her forever, but I did none of those things. I allowed myself to be led down the corridor and out of the station. I did not look back. For thirty years I've wished I had, that I'd made that final glimpse, said that silent goodbye.

The rest is a blur of raised voices, telephone calls, indignation. *Wild* and *out of control* and *delinquent* and *criminal record* were words I heard again and again, some directed at me, some shouted into the phone at my parents. *Liar. Crazy.* I never returned to the school. I spent two days under virtual house arrest, imposed by Frank and Louise, hardly able to leave my room. I slept a great deal. Again and again I ran to the toilet and vomited, my body seemingly ripping itself to pieces from the inside. At night I entertained a vague hope that Lucy would tap at my window again, that we would try running away again, maybe on foot this time—running to the ocean, to the dunes, the sea. Living on our own. Stealing food, sleeping under the stars, far from adults and their poisonous lives. *Please come, Lucy. Please come.* But she didn't, and I certainly couldn't; it was not in my personality to lead.

On the third morning, my bags packed, Uncle Frank impatiently warming up the car in the driveway to take me back to the bus station, to my parents whom I no longer wanted to see or know (and who would soon be serving sentences for narcotics possession with intent to distribute and various tax evasion charges while I languished in a series of foster homes), I saw the headline.

LOCAL GIRL MISSING. Below it, a photograph of Lucy.

Much later, when I learned the truth, I thought: *She went without me.*

She left me alone.

Lucy, I said to myself thousands of times, why didn't you ask me? Why didn't you tap on my window? I would have gone with you there. To his basement. I would. I would have gone anywhere with you, Lucy, anywhere and forever, Lucy, Lucy.

Nightmares then, sometimes even now. Screaming. Darkness. Sounds of drills and saws, wet sounds. Horrible bloody violations.

The remainder of my adolescence lost in blackout. Not thinking of Lucy, not thinking of anything. My mother released when I was eighteen, my father two years later. Occasional calls. Telephones slammed down. I never heard from Frank or Louise again, and have never returned to that town, never driven on that freeway, never gone to that beach. I live on the other side of the country. I will die without ever seeing those things again; they are hardly even part of my memory now. They inhabit my dream world, drifting meaninglessly among all things that never were, and could not be.

And yet, at some point, light. Breath. Life, continuing.

The Riverbed Killer lives, though he is dead. He inhabits cyberspace now, immortalized in word and image, floating everywhere, all around us, never to be escaped forever. And Lucy too, trapped there with him, in the silent interstices between bits of what we choose to call the world. And discovering her, them: impulsively typing in *Lucy Sparrow*, a name I had not thought of in years, not expecting to locate anything yet instantaneously finding her face, a face I once touched softly in darkness, now frozen behind the glowing glass of a computer monitor. Present even when I click out of the website, she is there, here, with him, all around us, always. Once they were both only locked away in files, on yellowing newsprint and police reports, buried.

Now…

I hear a car pull up in the driveway and rush from my study. I see them there, the two of them. My husband and daughter. I run to her, pull her to me, frightening her with my intensity but I cannot seem to hold back. I whisper, "You're home, you're home, thank God you're *home*," and my daughter, twelve-going-on-thirteen, returns the embrace, looking up at me, asking breathlessly, "Mom, what is it? Did I do something wrong? Why are you crying? Mom?"

About the Author

CHRISTOPHER CONLON is the author of a previous novel, *Midnight on Mourn Street,* which he recently adapted for the stage. His poetry has been published widely and collected in four books, the most recent of which is *Starkweather Dreams.* As an editor his credits include *Poe's Lighthouse, The Twilight Zone Scripts of Jerry Sohl,* and the Bram Stoker Award-winning *He Is Legend: An Anthology Celebrating Richard Matheson.* Conlon lives in Silver Spring, Maryland. Visit him online at

www.christopherconlon.com

www.ingramcontent.com/pod-product-compliance
Lightning Source LLC
Chambersburg PA
CBHW070817180626
46818CB00001B/301